THE CARTER FILE

AN AUNT BESSIE COLD CASE MYSTERY

DIANA XARISSA

Copyright © 2021 DX Dunn, LLC
Cover Photo Copyright © 2019 Kevin Moughtin

ISBN: 9798570297623
All Rights Reserved

❦ Created with Vellum

AUTHOR'S NOTE

We've already reached the third book in this new series. I hope you are enjoying reading them as much as I'm enjoying writing them.

As ever, I've used British English terms and spelling, although I'm certain I'm making more mistakes now than I did formerly. The longer I'm in the US, the more likely it is that errors will creep in. Please let me know if you find any so that I can correct them in future books.

This is a work of fiction and all of the characters are the fictional creations of the author. Any resemblance they may have to any real persons, living or dead, is entirely coincidental. The businesses named throughout the book are also fictional and again, if they resemble any real businesses, on the island or elsewhere, that is also coincidental. The historical sites mentioned within the book are all real, but the events that happen within them in the story are fictional.

Please don't hesitate to get in touch. I love hearing from readers. All of my contact details are available in the back of the book.

CHAPTER 1

The knock on the door surprised Elizabeth Cubbon. She wasn't expecting any visitors on the last day of November. It was cold and wet outside the window, and she couldn't imagine that anyone had come to see her to admire her view of the beach, either.

"Harry?" she said questioningly as she opened the door to someone completely unexpected.

"Miss Cubbon, good afternoon," Harry Blake replied. "I hope I'm not interrupting anything important?"

"Call me Bessie," she said automatically as she tried to work out what the man could possibly want.

Harry was a retired Scotland Yard inspector who worked on Andrew Cheatham's cold case unit with Bessie. He was a tall man, with dark hair streaked with grey. His eyes were dark as well and, to Bessie, they seemed to belong to a much older man, one who had seen many horrible things in his lifetime. The pair had barely spoken, though, over the past two months since the unit had begun meeting. Harry lived in London and came to the island for a week each month only for their meetings. He stayed at the Seaview Hotel in Ramsey while he was there and, as far as Bessie had known, he didn't even know where she lived.

Of course, she'd lived on the Isle of Man for a great many years. Nearly anyone on the island could have told Harry where to find "Aunt Bessie's" cottage.

He smiled. "Thank you, Bessie."

"And do come in," she added, realising that he'd been standing in the rain while she'd been lost in thought.

"Thank you again," Harry said. He stepped carefully into the cottage and then slowly looked around the room.

Bessie watched his face as he studied her cosy kitchen. He seemed to be taking in every single detail, and Bessie found herself wondering when she'd last scrubbed the top of her refrigerator. No doubt Harry had catalogued exactly how much dust had gathered there since she'd last cleaned.

"Have a seat," she said after an awkward pause. She waved at the small table in the corner of the room. There were four chairs around it, including the one Bessie had been sitting on when the man had knocked. She'd left her book of logic puzzles open on the table when she'd answered the door.

Harry took a few steps towards the table and then looked back at her. "I've interrupted your logic puzzle," he said. "I am sorry."

She shrugged. "I couldn't work it out anyway. I should just stop when I get about halfway through the book. That's usually where the puzzles begin to get too difficult for me."

"I've never tried them," he said as he dropped into the chair opposite the one Bessie had been using. "I never seem to have the time."

"I thought you were retired."

"I am, in theory, but I do quite a lot of consulting work. It keeps me busy, and I still enjoy it. If I'm honest, I miss working."

Thanks to a small inheritance at eighteen, Bessie had

never held down a paying job. Over the years, she'd filled her time with a great deal of volunteer work, but the small sum that she was being paid for taking part in the cold case unit was the first time she'd ever received a pay cheque. It was difficult, therefore, for her to understand what Harry missed about working.

"I should think you'd enjoy being able to do whatever you want all the time," she replied as she walked to the sink. "Tea?"

"Tea would be much appreciated, thank you. I've never really had any hobbies. I loved my job, and it's pretty much what I want to do all the time," he told her.

While Bessie waited for the kettle to boil, she got down a box of biscuits and arranged some on a plate. After putting that on the table, she added smaller plates for each of them and then made the tea. As she sat down in her chair, she shut the logic puzzle book and pushed it to one side.

"Thank you," Harry said as he took a few biscuits and put them on his plate.

"But what can I do for you?" Bessie asked, feeling as if she'd only just managed to avoid blurting out the question every second since the man had arrived.

"We've considered two cases thus far in the cold case unit," Harry replied after a sip of tea. "And your input has been key to both solutions. I want to get to know you better. I want to learn more about everyone on the team, actually."

"Everyone?" Bessie echoed, not certain what the man was after.

"When we started, Andrew told us to expect that we'd solve about ten per cent of our cases. I thought he was being optimistic. I've been involved in these sorts of units before, and we've never solved even five per cent of our cases. With this unit, we're two for two, and I want to understand why.

You and your friends work well together. I want you to tell me all about all of you."

Bessie took a sip of tea and then slowly ate a biscuit while she tried to think. It wasn't that she didn't want to tell the man about herself and her friends, exactly. She just didn't enjoy feeling as if she didn't have a choice. "I see," she said eventually.

"I know that we all introduced ourselves at the first meeting, but I had other things on my mind at that time, and I don't really recall what was said. I've tapped a few sources to get some basic facts, but I want to learn more. Obviously, how much you tell me is entirely up to you," Harry added. "I'd love to hear more about the island, as well. I'd never been here before the first meeting, and I'm surprised by how lovely it is, actually."

"I'm glad you feel that way. When Andrew first told me about the cold case unit and mentioned that you and Charles were going to be a part of it, he suggested that he might meet with you two in London and the rest of us here. I think it works better if we're all together, though."

Harry nodded. "I might not come over every month, but for now I've been able to fit the meetings into my schedule. It helps that we're meeting early this month. Things get crazy around Christmas."

"Indeed. I'm involved with a charity fundraiser that starts in the middle of the month. I'm not certain that I'd be able to attend the meetings if they were much later in December. And I've a wedding to go to at the end of the month, as well."

"What sort of charity fundraiser?"

"It's called Christmas at the Castle. It's held at Castle Rushen in Castletown. Different charities from around the island each decorate a room in the castle for Christmas, and then the public can buy tickets to see the beautiful decorations. The visitors get to vote for their favourites, and all of the charities share the proceeds from ticket sales and also from an auction on the last evening," Bessie explained.

"I saw the castle from the outside when I drove around the island, but I haven't visited it properly. It looked to be a substantial medieval fortress."

"It is, indeed. It was a prison for many years, and now it's a museum, although some parts are still used for other things."

"There's also a castle in Peel, although that one didn't look as well maintained."

Bessie laughed. "Peel Castle is mostly in ruins. There are a few standing structures, but the entire site is a heritage site. I highly recommend a visit to both castles, though, if you can find the time."

Harry glanced out the window at the heavy rain. "Maybe in the spring," he told her.

"Actually, both castles are closed at the moment anyway, although I reckon I could get someone to show you around if you really wanted to see them now."

"You have connections with whoever owns the castles?"

"They're owned by Manx National Heritage, and I've done volunteer work with them for many years."

"How many years?"

Bessie flushed. "Since it was founded in the early fifties, actually."

"And you've lived on the island for your entire life?"

"My entire adult life, yes, but not my entire life," Bessie replied. She took a sip of tea while she considered how much she wanted to tell the man. Her life story was well known on the island, of course. Harry could ask just about anyone about her and probably be told more than she'd really care for him to know. Some of it would be untrue, of course, but the island's gossips didn't worry much about keeping the facts straight, not if some embellishments made for a better story.

She sighed. "I was born on the island, but my parents decided to move to America when I was two. We settled near Cleveland, Ohio, where other family members were already living. When I was seventeen, they decided that we were going to move back."

"That must have been difficult for you. Surely you didn't remember anything about the island. Ohio was all that you'd ever known."

"That's very true," Bessie replied. "I didn't want to leave the US. It was home for me, and I'd also met a man, one that I was convinced was the only man in the world for me."

"Since you're here, I'm going to guess that your parents wouldn't let you stay behind in the US."

"No, they would not. My older sister was engaged to a man she'd been seeing for several years. They got married very quickly, and she stayed in the US with him. My parents refused to give me permission to marry Matthew Saunders, the man I loved. I was only seventeen, and they wouldn't hear of my staying behind with a man they barely knew."

"So they dragged you back to the island?"

"They did," Bessie agreed. She hesitated for a moment and then decided that she might as well tell him the rest of the story. "Matthew wrote to me a short while later to tell me that he was coming to get me. Unfortunately, he didn't survive the sea journey. He passed away shortly before the ship docked in Liverpool," she said. Even after so many years, Bessie had to blink several times and swallow hard to keep her emotions in check.

"I'm sorry," Harry said after a moment.

"It was a long time ago. Matthew left me all of his worldly goods. I had enough money to buy this cottage, with a bit left over. My very clever advocate invested the extra money on my behalf and, thanks to him, I've lived off of that money ever since."

"He must have been very clever."

She nodded. For many years, she'd lived her life expecting to be told at any time that the money had run out, but instead, her investments had continued to grow. After living very frugally for such a long time, she was now at a point in her life where she could truly spoil herself. For Bessie, that meant buying hardcover books instead of waiting for the paperback versions to be released. Beyond that, she was quite content in her little cottage by the sea, and she knew that one day her relatives in America would be pleasantly surprised by the size of their inheritance from her.

"So you bought this cottage when you were eighteen?" Harry asked, looking around the kitchen again.

"I did. I've had two extensions added, and I had the kitchen remodelled in the late fifties. I can't imagine that I'll do anything further with it now that I've settled into middle age."

Harry stared at her for a moment and then nodded very slowly. "I wasn't going to ask your age," he said.

"It's none of your business," she replied tartly. "I stopped keeping track of my age when I got my free bus pass. When I get a birthday card from the Queen, well, then I'll know I've turned one hundred, but until then, I'm not counting."

"That's very wise, actually. And you've never been married?"

"There was another man who once suggested that we might marry, but I turned him down. He lived in Australia, and I wasn't interested in leaving the island."

Harry nodded. "Tell me about your friends," he requested. "The ones in the cold case unit, I mean. I'm not expecting you to tell me their deepest, darkest secrets, but I really want to hear how you all became friends. You don't seem to have much in common."

Bessie nodded. "We don't, really, I suppose. But I don't even know where to start." She picked up her teacup and frowned at it. "I need more tea," she told Harry. After she'd poured them each a second cup of tea and added a few more biscuits to the plate, she sat back down.

"Let's start with Hugh. I've known him the longest," she suggested.

"Constable Hugh Watterson, mid-twenties, married to Grace, one child, a daughter called Alice," Harry said.

"His daughter is Aalish," Bessie corrected him.

"Can you spell that for me?"

Bessie laughed and complied. "It's the Manx form of Alice, so you weren't too far off," she added.

"But I was wrong," he said with a frown. "I'm going to have to go back through my notes and see if I got bad information or simply remembered it incorrectly. But you were saying…"

"I've known Hugh since he was a child. Laxey Beach is a popular place for children to play in the summer months. It was even more popular before the holiday cottages were built."

Just past Bessie's cottage was a long row of small holiday cottages. Thomas and Maggie Shimmin had purchased the homes that had been there for decades and then torn them down to make space for their holiday rentals. The beach itself was still open to the public, but in the summer months, when the cottages were full of holidaymakers, there was limited room for Laxey families to come and enjoy the sand and the sea.

"And Hugh used to play on the beach?" Harry asked.

"He spent as much time down here as he could," Bessie replied, remembering the small boy who used to race up and down the sand, seemingly unable to use up all of his energy.

"And do you often speak to the children on the beach?" Harry asked.

"As I've never had children of my own, I've always been something of an honorary aunt to the boys and girls in Laxey," Bessie explained. "Many of them used to enjoy coming to my cottage for biscuits during their time at the beach. Once they became teenagers, they saw my cottage as a safe place where they could come if they were having problems with their parents. I have a spare bedroom, and I used to allow teenagers to spend the night when things were difficult at home."

"You're speaking as if that no longer happens."

Bessie frowned. "Over the past three years, I've been involved in a number of murder investigations. As a result, parents have become increasingly reluctant to allow their children to stay with me. At times I miss having children and teenagers around, but I do enjoy having my cottage all to myself, as well."

"But we were talking about Hugh."

"We were. His parents didn't approve of his desire to join the police, so he took to spending quite a lot of his time here during his teen years. His parents are both incredibly proud of him now, though, and I know they adore Aalish."

"So you and Hugh have been friends since he was a child."

"I've known him since he was a child. We became friends the first time I stumbled over a dead body. He was the first constable on the scene that awful day nearly three years ago."

"How long have you known the others, then?"

"I met Doona Moore nearly five years ago now."

"Ah, Mrs. Moore," he said. "You'll probably tell me that I've something wrong with what I know about her, too. She's in her mid-forties. She's been married twice, divorced once, and widowed once. When her second husband died, he left her a considerable fortune, although she's had some difficulty getting her hands on it due to legal complications. I believe she's wealthy enough now that she's stopped working, although she was formerly a receptionist at the Laxey Constabulary. I also believe that she and John Rockwell are, um, a couple."

"I suppose all of that is correct, although it sounds odd when simply listed in that way. I met Doona at a Manx language class. I was taking it for the third time, but it was her first attempt."

"I understand Celtic languages are very difficult."

"They are, at least for me. I've taken the class multiple times and I still can't say much more than *moghrey mie*."

"Which means?"

"Good morning, and it isn't even morning," Bessie laughed. "Anyway, I met Doona in the class. She'd signed up hoping to meet single men, but she was far and away the youngest person there. Her second marriage was falling apart at that point, and I did my best to help her through what was a very difficult time for her."

"And you've been friends ever since," Harry concluded for her.

"We have, through multiple murder investigations, including that of her second husband."

"So when did you meet John Rockwell? I know he's the police inspector in charge of the Laxey Constabulary. He was with the police in Manchester before he moved to the island. He's in his mid-forties and divorced, although his former wife, Susan, passed away nearly a year ago. They had two children, Thomas and Amy, who now live with John. I believe they're both in their teens."

"That's all correct, although I'm not entirely certain that John's wife was actually Susan. I've only ever heard her called

Sue. Of course, that's a nickname for Susan, but it doesn't have to be."

Harry nodded. "I'll check my sources."

What sources? Bessie wondered. "I met John over that same dead body that I mentioned earlier, the first one that I was unfortunate enough to discover. He was the inspector put in charge of the investigation and, over the years since, we've become friends."

"Interesting," Harry said. "And how did you meet Andrew?"

Bessie smiled. "In the middle of another murder investigation, actually, at a holiday park in the UK. It was Doona's second husband who'd turned up dead. Andrew simply happened to be staying in the cabin next to the one that Doona and I were sharing. We started talking and, eventually, we were able to work together to help the police solve the case."

"And based on that, Andrew invited you to be a part of the cold case unit?"

"We stayed in touch after we'd both returned home. Andrew came to visit some months later and, while he was here, he told me about a cold case. Again we were able to work together to solve the case. According to him, that was where the idea for the cold case unit first arose."

"Really?" Harry glanced at his watch and then got to his feet. "As fascinating as this has been, I'm afraid I have an appointment elsewhere. Thank you very much for your time."

Bessie walked him to the door. "I'll see you at the meeting tomorrow," she said.

"Yes, I'm looking forward to it. Andrew said it's murder again," Harry replied.

Bessie watched as he crossed the small parking area outside of her cottage. His car was the only one there, a small black car with a large orange sticker that identified which hire car company owned it. Harry waved as he drove away.

"But what did he want?" Bessie asked as she cleared away the cups and plates. She felt as if she'd told him a great deal about herself and her friends, but the more she thought about it, the more she realised that she'd learned nothing about him. Frowning, she sat back down with her logic puzzle book and pencil. *Tomorrow, when Andrew arrives, I'll ask him about Harry,* she decided.

CHAPTER 2

"I don't know what I can tell you," Andrew said as they made their way to Ramsey the next afternoon. His flight had been delayed, so he'd made it to Laxey only just in time to collect Bessie before the meeting.

"He said he wanted to understand why our unit had had so much early success," Bessie told him.

"And you didn't believe him?"

"I don't know what to think," Bessie sighed. "I simply feel as if I told him a great deal and got nothing back in return."

"He's a police inspector. He's spent his entire life interrogating witnesses. I'm fairly certain he doesn't talk about himself to anyone."

"So what can you tell me about him?"

"Not much. He's in his sixties, retired, and he was very good at his job, which was investigating murders. He had a reputation for being especially good at the most gruesome and horrific of them, but that might have been at least partly because he was willing to take on those types of cases where others might have shied away, given a choice."

"I didn't think police inspectors got much choice."

"In a large homicide division, inspectors can, to some extent, influence which cases they get assigned. I never volunteered to take on the more gory murders, although I always did my best with them when they were assigned to me."

"And Harry volunteered for them?"

"He did. And the more he solved, the more he was assigned."

"What about his personal life?"

"He's never been married. Beyond that, I know nothing."

Bessie frowned. "I should have asked him about himself."

"It sounds very much as if he ended the conversation once he'd learned what he wanted to know," Andrew told her. "He's a very private person. I doubt he would have answered your questions even if you'd managed to ask any."

Andrew drove into the large car park for the Seaview and found a space near the door.

"It's very quiet here, isn't it?" he asked as he led Bessie to the entrance.

"I believe it's always quiet in the winter months," Bessie replied as they walked into the huge and beautifully decorated foyer.

"We've quite a few bookings for Christmas," Jasper Coventry, the hotel's owner and manager who was standing behind the reception desk, told them. "I'm starting to think that no one wants to stay with his or her family during the holidays."

Andrew laughed. "I shall be booking myself into a bed and breakfast near my daughter's house. I love her and all of my children and grandchildren and great-grandchildren, but I don't want to stay with any of them, not even for a single night, not even on Christmas."

Jasper grinned at him. "That sort of attitude is good news

for the hospitality industry, anyway," he said. "But how are you both today?"

"I'm very well, thank you," Bessie replied.

"I'm a bit frazzled, as my flight was delayed and I very nearly didn't make it to my own meeting," Andrew told him.

Jasper glanced up at the clock. "And now I'm making you late," he said. "I do apologise. I believe everyone else is already here."

"Where are we meeting today?" Bessie asked.

"I've put you in the main conference room," Jasper replied. "It's a bit larger than the ones I typically have you use, but I want to keep moving you around, just in case anyone is snooping."

Bessie nodded. Dan Ross, the most annoying man in the world, at least in Bessie's opinion, was endlessly curious as to why Bessie and her friends were meeting regularly with three former Scotland Yard inspectors. Dan was an investigative journalist for the local newspaper, and, in his opinion, he needed to know about everything that happened on the island. Andrew preferred that no one know about the cold case unit, so Jasper was doing his best to move them around the hotel in an effort to hide just how often they were gathering.

Jasper led them down a long corridor to the very last room. When he opened the door, five heads turned and whatever conversation had been happening stopped.

"I'm sorry we're late," Andrew said as he and Bessie walked inside. "My flight was delayed."

"Grab a cuppa before you sit down," Doona suggested, giving Bessie a warm smile.

Doona's brown hair looked as if it had been recently cut and styled. The highlights that ran through it seemed more subtle than usual, and Bessie was fairly certain that her friend had found a new and probably quite expensive salon.

Her clothes were nicer than the jeans and casual tops that she typically wore, as well, and Bessie wondered if Doona was finally starting to appreciate the wealth that she'd inherited. When their eyes met, Bessie noticed that Doona's usual bright green contact lenses had been replaced by a much softer green. It was even possible that what she was seeing was Doona's own natural eye colour, she thought as she poured herself some tea.

Jasper always provided a great deal of delicious food, and Bessie couldn't stop herself from filling a plate with miniature cakes, biscuits, and other treats. Andrew was still shuffling papers when she slid into a seat next to him.

"How are you?" John asked her as she took a bite of cake.

His green eyes were natural, or so Bessie assumed, as both of his children had them as well. Brown hair with hints of grey made him look distinguished. Bessie considered him one of the handsomest men she'd ever met, and he was also one of the kindest.

"I'm very well, thanks," she replied, glancing up and down the table. "How's the baby?" she asked Hugh.

"She's going to have a birthday soon," Hugh replied, sounding slightly dazed by the idea. "It doesn't seem possible."

Bessie laughed. "Babies do grow up into children, and then teenagers and even adults," she reminded him. And she knew it was true, too, even if Hugh still looked to be only around fifteen to her. His brown hair usually appeared as if it needed to be cut, and he always seemed to be trying and failing to grow a moustache. He was considerably taller than Bessie, but then, nearly everyone towered over her, as she wasn't much over five feet tall. Hugh and John were both around a foot taller, although Doona was closer to her height.

"Charles, how are you?" Andrew asked.

The grey-haired man looked up from his mobile phone and nodded at Andrew. "Fine, busy, same as always."

Bessie knew that Charles, who'd been an expert at locating missing people during his years with the police, was in great demand as a consultant on missing person cases all over the world. She kept expecting him to quit the cold case unit, as it seemed to take up more time than he seemed interested in devoting to it.

"Let's get started then," Andrew suggested. "Jeff in New York sent a lengthy email, thanking all of you for your part in helping to apprehend Leon," he said, referring to their previous investigation.

"It's good that he's behind bars," Doona said. "But I do feel sorry for Anja."

"According to Jeff, she's now involved with one of the policemen who interviewed her recently," Andrew replied.

Doona chuckled. "She deserves a happy ending."

Andrew nodded. "Time to move on. We're doing something different this time. Another murder, but one in which there is a limited list of possible suspects. It's similar to a case that Bessie once helped me solve, but, in that case, the key was finding out that the victim had been misidentified. That is definitely not the case here."

He stopped to pass around large envelopes to each of them. Bessie opened hers and pulled out the thick case file.

"Before you start reading, let me walk you through the case," Andrew interjected. "I probably should have waited to give you those until after I'd done so, really, but I thought you'd want to look at the crime scene photos."

As everyone began to turn pages, he laughed.

"Let's leave that for a moment, though, if you don't mind. Let me give you the basics," he said.

Bessie shut her folder and opened her notebook. Pen in hand, she looked over at Andrew.

He waited until everyone was paying attention before he began. "On the first Friday in June, 1985, the senior class of Greenview High School in Greenview, Pennsylvania, graduated. That evening, six of the new graduates went off to a cottage by a nearby lake to celebrate their achievement. By all accounts, they spent most of the weekend drinking heavily. On Sunday morning, when the first member of the group woke up, she found one of the other young women dead in the living room of the cottage."

Bessie frowned. "How sad," she murmured.

"And the police are certain that one of the other five killed her?" Harry asked.

"As certain as they can be. The cottage was quite isolated, and it had rained heavily all weekend. The only tyre tracks along the road that led to the cottage belonged to the vehicles that the six of them had used to get out there. The group hadn't been outside of the cottage since they'd arrived on the Friday evening, and there weren't any footprints in the mud around the cottage."

"Tell us about all six of the young people," John suggested.

"They were in couples," Andrew told him. "I'll start with Harvey Light and Mary Ellen Baxter. The cottage belonged to Mary Ellen's parents, and they were the ones who'd stocked it with food and a great deal of alcohol. They reasoned that the kids would be safe enough, as no one would be driving or bothering anyone out there in the middle of nowhere."

"What was the legal drinking age in Pennsylvania in 1985?" John asked.

"Twenty-one," Andrew told him.

"So they were happy providing alcohol to minors," John remarked. "Assuming that students in the US graduate high school before they turn twenty-one, that is."

Andrew nodded. "The six men and women involved were

all either eighteen or nineteen. As for the underage drinking, that was a problem for the local police at the time. I don't believe that it's relevant to the murder."

"So tell us about Harvey and Mary Ellen," Harry said.

"Harvey was the oldest. He'd turned nineteen in January. He was the quarterback on the football team and had been homecoming king, whatever that is. Apparently he was very popular. His father was a lawyer, and his mother was a stay-at-home mom to him and a younger sister who was a year behind him in school," Andrew told them.

"So they had money?" Harry asked.

"They did. Harvey had been accepted to one of the Ivy League schools and was expected to follow in his father's footsteps. You'll be able to read it for yourself, but his mother commented that prior to the murder her biggest worry had been that her son might get a girl pregnant and ruin his future."

"Murder is a good deal more serious than an unplanned pregnancy," Doona remarked.

"But it may well have had less impact on his future," Harry pointed out.

Andrew nodded. "Let me tell you about everyone involved. I've given you their initial statements and the results of the police investigation. I've deliberately not given you any recent updates on the five suspects. I want you to read the case file and give me your thoughts on what you've read before I share the recent updates the police in Pennsylvania gave me."

Bessie frowned. The last case they'd worked on had been largely solved once they'd discovered what had happened to the various suspects in the time since the murder.

"I will point out that there's nothing in what the suspects are currently doing that points to a clearly guilty party in the murder," Andrew added. "If there were, we wouldn't be considering the case."

"So Harvey was a spoiled rich kid," Doona said. "Who else was there?"

"His girlfriend, Mary Ellen, had a similar background. Her father was actually in partnership with Harvey's father, and her mother was a vice president at one of the local banks. They had a large home in the centre of town, plus the cottage on the lake, and another vacation home in the Poconos where they went skiing several times each winter," Andrew told them.

"How nice for them," Hugh muttered.

"Mary Ellen had been head cheerleader at the high school and had been accepted to a small, all-female liberal arts college. She was going to study history and English, with plans to go to law school after her first degree," Andrew told them. "Her mother was quite clear that the family expected her and Harvey to both return to Greenview to work with their fathers and to one day take over the law firm. She also suggested that both families wanted the pair to get married, but Harvey's mother seemed less keen on the idea."

"She was worried about Harvey getting Mary Ellen pregnant," Charles suggested.

"Possibly. Her comment, when asked, was more along the lines of them both being too young to make such a serious commitment at that point," Andrew replied.

"She was quite right about that," Bessie said.

Andrew nodded. "Anyway, that's our first couple."

"And she wasn't the victim, I assume," Bessie replied.

"She was not. The next couple is Jack Morton and Katie Dawson. Jack's father was a doctor. He was a local pediatrician, actually, and when interviewed he remarked that he'd looked after every single one of the six people who'd been at the cottage when they'd been children."

"I'm going to assume that his family had money, too, then," Doona said.

"Some, but not as much as Harvey's and Mary Ellen's," Andrew told her. "Jack's mother was also a stay-at-home mother, but she had six children to look after. At the time of the murder, they ranged in age from twenty-one to six."

"That's quite a range," Charles remarked.

"Where did Jack fit into the family?" Bessie asked.

"He was the third child of the six. He'd been accepted to a state-run university where he was hoping to study biology so that he could eventually go to medical school," Andrew told her. "Katie's father was a college professor at the local community college. Her mother worked as a teaching assistant at an elementary school."

"It sounds as if her family wasn't in the same league financially as the others," Harry said.

"They were not. Katie admitted as much in her interview. She said she couldn't quite believe it when Jack had first shown interest in her, and that she still wasn't used to hanging out with the most popular kids at school."

"What was she planning to do next?" Hugh asked.

"She'd been given a very generous scholarship to a private liberal arts college. According to her statement, she wanted to teach high school maths once she'd finished."

"Why would anyone want to teach maths?" Hugh wondered.

"How long had she and Jack been seeing one another?" Doona asked.

"About three months. And before you ask, Harvey and Mary Ellen had been a couple since middle school, which, I'm told, means that they'd been together for five or six years by that point," Andrew said.

"No wonder Harvey's mother was worried," Charles said.

"And Katie wasn't the victim?" Bessie wondered.

"No, but she was the unfortunate one who found the body," Andrew told her.

Bessie shuddered. She'd had far too much experience with finding dead bodies. It was incredibly unsettling, and she'd been considerably older when she'd found her first one. Finding one at eighteen must have been traumatic.

"And the last couple?" John asked.

"Mike Beam and Julie Carter," Andrew told him. "Mike's father worked as an assistant manager at a local factory, and his mother worked at the local supermarket. They definitely weren't in the same social circle, but Mike was apparently an amazing football player. He'd earned himself a football scholarship to a good college, and he and Harvey were friends, which is why he was invited along to the cottage by the lake."

"And Julie?" Bessie asked, already feeling sorry for the young woman who she knew was the victim of murder.

"She was eighteen. Her father was a heart surgeon and very highly respected in his field. He spent much of his time travelling around the country, lecturing about the subject. Her mother, well, let's just say that the police had difficulty interviewing her, as she was rarely sober enough to answer their questions. I'll add that that included when they went to speak to her just after the murder, before she'd been given the news. It wasn't losing her daughter that drove her to drink. Julie was an only child, and she was planning to go to California for college. Mike told the police that she'd wanted to get as far away from her mother and father as she possibly could."

"The poor girl," Bessie said softly.

"And then she was murdered by one of her friends," Doona said.

"How long had she been involved with Mike?" John asked.

"About two months," Andrew told him. "Mike told the police that it wasn't anything serious, but Mary Ellen told

THE CARTER FILE

them that Julie was crazy about Mike and was hoping to marry him one day."

"They were all so very young," Bessie sighed.

"And I want you to keep that in mind as you read what they told the police in their interviews," Andrew told them. "As I said, I've given you copies of those interviews, as well as copies of the interviews with all six sets of parents. There are a few other reports in there as well, from talks that the police had with teachers from the school and with the football coach. I want you to read through them all, and then come back ready to discuss what you think happened in that cottage on the lake."

"And then you'll tell us where everyone is now?" Bessie demanded.

Andrew nodded. "We'll meet again the day after tomorrow. I want to give you all plenty of time to read through the file."

"That's Sunday," Hugh said. "At the same time?"

"Yes, unless that doesn't work for anyone?"

No one objected. "You can take a look at the crime scene photos if you'd like," he said.

Bessie flipped open the folder and shuffled through the pages. She stopped when she reached the first photograph. The pretty blonde girl looked as if she might be sleeping. The huge knife in her chest and the enormous amount of blood surrounding her told the rest of the story, though.

"Whoever killed her must have been covered in blood," Harry said.

"The cabin was thoroughly searched. No bloody clothing was ever recovered," Andrew told him.

"There aren't any footprints in the blood, either. It's almost as if she lay down on the couch and stabbed herself," Hugh said.

"The coroner determined that there was no way the

injuries could have been self-inflicted," Andrew replied. "He suggested that it was possible that the wound hadn't bled immediately, that maybe the killer had just enough time to jump away before Julie began to slowly bleed to death."

Bessie drew a deep breath and then blinked back tears. Whatever had happened, she felt tremendous sympathy for the young girl in the pictures. Julie deserved justice after all these years. Bessie could only hope she and the rest of the unit could help get it for her.

CHAPTER 3

"If that's all for today, I'll see you on Sunday, then," Harry said as he got to his feet.

Charles quickly stood up as well. "Yes, until Sunday," he muttered, staring at his mobile phone as he grabbed his envelope and left the room.

Harry followed him out. As the door swung shut behind them, Bessie looked at the others. "Do you want to meet tomorrow night to discuss the case?" she asked them.

"Yes, please," Doona said as John nodded.

"If I can get my homework done, I'll be there," Hugh told her. Bessie knew he was working hard at the local college, taking classes that would one day lead to the degree that he needed if he was to ever be promoted to inspector.

"We'll bring dinner," John said.

"And I'll make something for pudding," Bessie replied.

"And I'll be there whether I have my homework done or not," Hugh added. "I'd much rather spend the time with all of you than doing maths."

"The homework is important, too," Bessie reminded him.

"But I'll have time on Sunday morning to get it done. It will be fine," Hugh insisted.

They all gathered up their copies of the reports and then headed for the exit as a group.

"Good afternoon," a familiar voice said from a corner of the foyer as they walked through it.

Bessie spun around and frowned at Dan Ross, who quickly crossed the room to her.

"How are you today?" he asked Bessie.

"Fine," she replied flatly.

"How was your meeting?" was Dan's next question.

Bessie sighed. "What brings you to the Seaview?" she asked.

"I might ask you the same question," he replied.

"Bessie, we're going to be late," Andrew said, putting a hand on Bessie's arm.

She smiled at him. "We're going to be late," she repeated to Dan before turning and walking briskly out of the building.

"He's following us," Doona whispered as they crossed the car park.

"He's welcome to follow us," John told her. "He can even take notes on what we buy at the shops, since that's where we're going next."

Everyone laughed, and then Doona and John got into John's car and drove away. Hugh wasn't far behind them. As Bessie climbed into Andrew's car, she glanced around. "He's in the black car on the far side of the car park," she told Andrew in a whisper.

"I don't think he can hear you from here," he teased as he started the car.

Bessie flushed. "Of course not," she said, feeling foolish.

"I hope you don't mind a slight detour on the way back to Laxey," Andrew added.

"Of course not. Where do you need to go?"

"Nowhere, but I thought it would be fun to let Mr. Ross follow us for a short while and then lose him."

"Do you really think he's going to try following us?"

"He already is, although I suppose he could simply be going in the same direction." Andrew drove to the end of the street and then made a series of random left and right turns. After a few minutes, he looked at Bessie. "He's definitely following us," he told her.

"What can we do?"

"Any number of things, but I think the simplest thing is to let him follow us to the nearest police station. I suspect that will scare him off."

Bessie gave him directions to the large station in Ramsey. As they approached the building, she watched Dan in the car's side mirror. Andrew slowed down and then indicated that he was turning into the station's car park. As Andrew turned, Dan drove past them, continuing down the street and then turning left and disappearing from view.

Andrew turned the car around and pulled back out of the car park. "Hopefully, that's him out of the way, for the day, at least."

They were back at Bessie's cottage a short while later.

"I know you have a friend coming over for dinner. I'll probably pop over in the morning," Andrew said as he parked the car.

The pair usually kept their arrangements for each day as casual as possible, as neither wanted to have to plan his or her life around the other. Bessie was a very early riser, and Andrew claimed that he was as well, but he tended to sleep late most mornings when he was on the island.

Inside her cottage, Bessie put the envelope Andrew had given her on the table in her sitting room. In the kitchen, she checked that she had everything she needed for the meal she was planning to prepare. It was important to her that she make something special for these particular guests.

Andy Caine was another young man who'd spent a great deal of time at Bessie's during his teen years. His mother had worked multiple jobs to make ends meet while his stepfather spent most of his time in the local pub. A few years earlier, Andy had learned the truth about his biological father. Unexpectedly, he'd inherited a small fortune from the family, money that had allowed him to pursue his dreams.

Having always wanted to be a chef and own his own restaurant, Andy had almost immediately gone across to the UK to attend culinary school. After two years of study, he'd come back to the island, and Bessie had been looking forward to the restaurant he was planning to open.

Many months had passed since his return, and Andy still hadn't found the right location for his restaurant. He was staying with his mother while he hunted for both that and a house, and it seemed to Bessie that he wasn't putting in nearly enough effort.

When he'd first returned to the island, he'd been romantically involved with Elizabeth Quayle, the youngest child of Bessie's friends George and Mary. Elizabeth had dropped out of several universities across before moving in with her parents at Thie yn Traie, the large mansion that sat on the cliff above Laxey Beach, just past the holiday cottages.

Bessie had thought that Andy and Elizabeth were well suited. Elizabeth had started the island's first party planning business and had often had Andy cater events for her. The pair had even been house-hunting together before someone from George's past was murdered.

Once the murderer was caught, George and Mary had decided to take an extended holiday, and they'd persuaded Elizabeth to go with them. Bessie wasn't certain how much persuasion it had taken, but, regardless, the trio, along with some staff, had been gone for over six months. The last Bessie had heard, they were due back at any moment, and it was possible that they had already returned to the island. If they had, though, Mary hadn't rung Bessie to let her know.

They are a concern for another day, Bessie thought. Tonight, she was entertaining Andy and the young woman now in his life, Jennifer Johnson. Jennifer had moved to the island about a year earlier to work for one of the local banks. Once Elizabeth had gone, though, Jennifer had opened her own party planning business. Bessie understood that Jennifer was doing very well, although Bessie had heard a few things about the woman that worried her.

When Bessie had last spoken to Andy, he'd announced that he and Jennifer were engaged, something that had surprised and concerned Bessie. He was meant to be bringing Jennifer with him to Bessie's that evening, and she was looking forward to meeting the woman.

It was too early to start cooking, so Bessie settled herself in the sitting room with her case file and a notebook. She carefully wrote the names of each of the six teenagers who'd been at the cabin by the lake on a separate sheet of paper. Later, after dinner, she'd start reading the interviews and taking notes. After a short while spent studying the photos of the cabin's exterior, including a look at the tyre tracks that led to the cabin, she put everything back in the envelope and headed for the kitchen.

A moment later, she returned to the sitting room. Feeling slightly foolish, she took the envelope and hid it under the cushions on the sofa. The contents were official police reports, after all. They were meant to be kept confidential. While she couldn't imagine either of her dinner guests opening the envelope even if he or she was alone in the sitting room, it was better to have it hidden, she decided.

Back in the kitchen, she went to work. An hour later,

everything was nearly ready, and Andy was five minutes late. Bessie found herself pacing back and forth as she watched the clock. Ten minutes later, just as she was thinking that everything was going to be ruined, someone knocked on the door.

"Andy, hello," she greeted the handsome young man.

"Hello," he replied. "I'm sorry we're late."

Bessie nodded. "I'm sure it couldn't be helped," she replied politely.

Andy stepped into the kitchen. The woman who followed him into the room was frowning.

"What does that say?" she asked, nodding at the sign just outside the door.

"Treoghe Bwaane," Bessie told her. "It's Manx for Widow's Cottage."

"You're a widow?" was the next question.

"No, the cottage already had the name when I bought it," Bessie explained.

The other woman looked around the small kitchen, and Bessie braced herself for what was sure to be a rude comment. Andy spoke quickly.

"Bessie Cubbon, this is Jennifer Johnson, my, er, fiancée. Jennifer, this is Bessie."

Jennifer nodded. "Yes, hello," she said, obviously not the least bit interested in meeting Bessie.

"Have a seat," Bessie suggested. "Let me get you something to drink before I serve dinner."

As Jennifer walked over to the table, Bessie studied her. Her blonde hair had dark roots. It had been pulled back into a low ponytail. Jennifer's eyes were green and she was slender. Bessie didn't care for the short skirt the woman was wearing or for the oversized jumper she'd put on over top of it. Jennifer dropped onto a chair and then gave Bessie a huge, fake smile.

"Andy's told me a lot about you," she said.

"I wish I could say the same," Bessie replied. "I'm looking forward to learning more about you over dinner. What can I get you to drink?"

"A glass of dry white wine," Jennifer replied.

Bessie flushed. "I'm sorry, but I don't have any wine."

"What do you have?" Jennifer asked.

Bessie ran through a list of options. When she was done, Jennifer looked at Andy and shrugged. "Whatever," she said.

"We'll both have coffee," Andy told Bessie. "And I can get it started if you want to serve dinner."

Andy had spent a great many hours in Bessie's kitchen over the years. He credited her for his love of cooking and baking, and she knew that he'd learned the basics from her. Knowing he was more than capable of making a pot of coffee, she got down plates and began to fill them.

"What is it?" Jennifer asked as Bessie put her plate on the table.

"Shepherd's pie," Bessie replied, feeling her cheeks flood with colour.

"I don't really eat..." Jennifer began.

"I'm sure it will be delicious," Andy interrupted. "Bessie taught me how to cook," he added.

Jennifer smiled tightly. "How nice."

With drinks and dinner on the table, Bessie sat down opposite Jennifer. "So, tell me about yourself. What brought you to the island?"

"My job," Jennifer replied. She took a tiny bite of her dinner and then chewed slowly.

"I believe someone mentioned that you used to work in banking," Bessie said after a moment.

"I did," Jennifer agreed, putting her fork down.

"But now you have a party planning business?" Bessie made the statement a question.

Jennifer nodded and then picked up her coffee cup.

"Do you enjoy party planning?" Bessie asked after an awkward pause.

"It's better than banking," Jennifer told her.

"Why?"

Jennifer stared at her for a moment and then shrugged. "I get to go to a lot of parties," she said eventually.

"I'm sure some of your customers are quite demanding, though," Bessie said, remembering some of the stories that Elizabeth had told her when she'd been running her business. "I'm told brides can be very difficult, for instance."

Jennifer shrugged. "I don't take difficult customers."

Bessie wanted to ask how that worked, but Andy interrupted before she could put the question into words.

"I've been looking at houses again," he told her.

"Really? How is it going?" Bessie asked.

"I had another look at the old Looney place. After everything that happened, the price had plummeted, but even so, I don't think I want to buy it."

"It's a disaster," Jennifer said. "No one in their right mind would buy it."

"It could be a beautiful home again," Bessie argued. "It was once one of the nicest homes in the village."

"And then it was left empty for decades until a man was murdered in the main bedroom," Jennifer replied. "It needs to be torn down and something lovely and modern needs to be built in its place."

"Is that something you'd consider doing?" Bessie asked Andrew.

He hesitated and then shook his head. "I don't want a modern home. I'm hoping to find something similar to the Looney mansion, but in better condition."

"In Laxey?" Bessie wondered.

"No," Jennifer said flatly.

Bessie looked at Andrew, who flushed. "Jennifer would rather live in Douglas," he explained.

"I'm sure you have a lot more options for properties in Douglas," Bessie said.

"Yes, but I still haven't found just the right place," Andy sighed.

"There are a lot of old hotels being converted into flats," Jennifer said. "We could get something right on the promenade. It would be modern on the inside, but old on the outside. It would be the perfect compromise."

Andy made a face. "I'd still prefer a detached house."

Jennifer rolled her eyes and didn't reply.

"If I hear of anything that might be coming on the market, I'll let you know," Bessie said. "What about the restaurant? If you want to live in Douglas, are you looking to have your restaurant there as well?"

"I'm not certain what I want to do about the business," Andy told her. "I'm even more particular about that, and I can't seem to find anything I like anywhere on the island."

"I want him to stop searching and simply cater for me," Jennifer interjected. "That would be far less work than a restaurant."

"But maybe not what Andy has always dreamt of doing," Bessie suggested.

Jennifer shrugged. She picked up her fork and pushed some of the food around on her plate.

"How have you been?" Andy asked Bessie. "It's been a while since you've been involved in any murder investigations, at least."

Bessie nodded. She wasn't meant to tell anyone about the cold case unit, after all. "I've been working on transcribing some diaries," she told the couple. "They belonged to a woman who used to live in Peel."

"Long ago?" Andy asked.

"The first diary starts in nineteen twenty," Bessie replied. "She was twenty years old."

"And what have you learned about her so far?" was Andy's next question.

"She's become rather obsessed with an apprentice blacksmith," Bessie told him. "I've read only the first five or six pages, but they're all about Harold Hartner. Apparently he was tall, dark, and handsome. From what I've read thus far, I don't believe the man even knows that young Carree exists, though."

"It doesn't sound as if that relationship is going anywhere," Andy suggested.

"It certainly doesn't seem to be, but I've four or five more books to get through. You never know," Bessie replied.

"Thank you for dinner," Jennifer said, pushing her still full plate of food towards the centre of the table. "I've a very busy day tomorrow. We probably should be going." She looked pointedly at Andy.

"You haven't had pudding," Bessie protested. "I made Andy's favourite shortbread."

Andy beamed at her. "Bessie's shortbread was one of the first things I learned how to bake," he told Jennifer. "And I've brazenly stolen her recipe and used it ever since."

Bessie laughed. "You're more than welcome to it," she assured him. She got up and cleared away the dinner dishes, tutting quietly to herself as she dumped Jennifer's meal into the rubbish bin. It took her only a moment to pile a plate high with slices of shortbread.

"More coffee?" she asked as she put the plate down on the table.

"We really can't stay," Jennifer said, grabbing a slice of shortbread and shoving it into her mouth.

Bessie frowned and then pulled out small plates for each of them to use with their pudding. Jennifer put hers on the table and then ignored it as she reached for more of the sweet treat. The second slice disappeared as quickly as the first had. Bessie wasn't surprised. The woman was probably starving, as she hadn't eaten her dinner.

"This was lovely," Jennifer said, getting to her feet as soon as the second piece of shortbread was gone. "Thank you."

Bessie stood up slowly, setting her own half-eaten piece of shortbread on the small plate in front of her. "I'm sorry you have to rush away so quickly," she said to Andy.

"Yes, well, Jennifer has been planning a luncheon for tomorrow, and there have been some last-minute issues. She's probably going to have to be up very early to make sure everything is sorted in time," Andy explained.

"The Seaview has let me down again," Jennifer said dramatically. "I really need to stop trying to have events there, as they have a nasty habit of cancelling on me at the last possible minute. Everyone on the island wants to have their events there, but they aren't at all reliable."

Bessie frowned. "Jasper Coventry, one of the owners, is a very dear friend of mine. I'm shocked that you've been having difficulties with him. He and his partner, Stuart, have worked incredibly hard to establish the Seaview as one of the island's most desirable locations. I can't imagine them cancelling events, especially not at this time of the year, when they aren't busy with guests."

Jennifer flushed. "It isn't Jasper who's been cancelling," she said quickly. "It's always someone from the catering staff who rings me. Maybe this time it was all a big misunderstanding, actually. I got a voicemail message that got cut off and I, well, I probably overreacted to it, and I may have been the one who cancelled everything."

"That wasn't what you told me before," Andy said, staring at Jennifer.

"I was upset before, and frazzled," Jennifer snapped. "The

details don't really matter anyway, not at this point. What matters now is that I have an event to put on tomorrow, which means I need an early night. Good night," she said to Bessie, heading for the door.

Andy was right behind her. "Good night," he said quickly, before he followed Jennifer out of the cottage.

"Good night," she muttered, staring after them. She watched as they climbed into Andy's car and he drove away.

Feeling as if the entire evening had been unsatisfactory, Bessie put the leftover shepherd's pie into the refrigerator and then sat down with another cup of coffee and some shortbread. The sweet treat did little to improve her mood, though. She hadn't cared for Jennifer, and she couldn't help but think that Andy deserved better.

Sighing, she went into the sitting room and pulled out the case file. It was time to start taking notes. Whatever the situation with Andy and Jennifer, poor Julie Carter deserved justice.

Two hours later, Bessie had short biographies of each of the six teenagers. She'd read the individual accounts of everything that had happened in the cabin by the lake, as well. It was far too early for her to identify the killer, but one of the suspects seemed more likely than the others, at least to her mind. With their stories still running through her head, she took herself off to bed.

WHEN HER INTERNAL alarm woke her at six the next morning, she was vaguely aware that she'd dreamt of groups of teenagers rushing up and down the beach. Sighing, she got out of bed and stood for a long time under a hot shower. The experience cleared her head, and by the time she'd made herself some toast and tea, she'd nearly forgotten her unsettling dreams.

A brisk walk on the beach, past Thie yn Traie, improved her mood even further. When she turned around and headed for home, she felt ready to get back to work on the investigation. She still had pages of interviews with the parents, teachers, coaches, and other men and women from the town to read. She hadn't read the crime scene reports yet, either. Then there was the autopsy to get through, something Bessie hated to even consider.

CHAPTER 4

Bessie was halfway through the rest of the interviews when someone knocked on the door. Aware that it could be Dan Ross, Bessie shoved all of the papers into a pile and then tucked them into a cupboard before she opened the door.

"Good morning," Andrew said brightly. "How are you today? Did you enjoy your dinner with your friend?"

"I'm fine, but I didn't exactly enjoy dinner. It was, well, it doesn't matter. How are you this morning?"

"I overslept again, but I can't complain. I have a terrible time falling asleep at home, and I never manage to sleep past five. Here, I have the opposite problem, and I feel so much better for being so well rested."

"Do you want to come in, or do you want to go out somewhere?" Bessie asked.

"How are you doing with the case file?" he wondered.

"Come in while we discuss it," Bessie suggested, looking up and down the beach. It was just possible that she was getting a bit paranoid about Dan, but she wasn't going to take any chances. If he did find out about the cold case unit, she didn't want to have been his source.

"I can make tea," Bessie offered once Andrew was settled at the table.

"Or we could go out somewhere," he suggested. "It's warm today for early December. I know the island has a great many walking trails, and I'm trying to get more exercise. How about a nice long walk, maybe with a pub lunch at the end of it?"

"That sounds good," Bessie said, feeling slightly surprised by the idea. Andrew was right, of course. The island had some wonderful walking trails, but she was so used to walking on the beach that she rarely took advantage of them. She changed into a warm jumper and then pulled on a heavy coat. It was warm for December, but it was still quite chilly outside. She had good, sturdy boots that were ideally suited for walking, but it took her a minute to find them. When she was ready, she and Andrew got into his car.

"If you've had time to read at least some of the case file, maybe we could talk about the suspects while we walk," Andrew suggested as he drove them towards Peel. They'd agreed to walk along the coast there, a route that Bessie had enjoyed walking years earlier.

"I'd like that. I'm still struggling to keep them all straight in my head, though," she replied.

"I brought my notes," Andrew told her, patting his coat pocket.

"I should have brought mine," Bessie said with a sigh.

A half hour later he found a parking space, and the pair got out of the car. A cold breeze made Bessie glad she'd worn her heavy coat. As she and Andrew made their way towards the coastal path, she heard someone calling her name.

"Dan Ross?" she said to Andrew. "What's he doing in Peel?"

"Good morning, Aunt Bessie," Dan said brightly when he reached them. "I wasn't expecting to see you here today."

"Likewise," Bessie replied.

"I thought Inspector Cheatham's friends were still at the Seaview," Dan said.

Bessie simply stared at him.

After a moment, Dan laughed. "So, what are you two planning for this morning?"

Bessie took in his light sweater and shiny black shoes and then smiled. "We're going to take a stroll along the coastal trail. Would you care to join us?"

Dan nodded and then frowned. "Trail?" he echoed.

Bessie gestured to the entrance to the path that was just visible ahead. "I thought we'd walk around behind Peel Castle," she told him.

"Ah, I don't suppose I'm dressed for that sort of hiking," Dan said.

Bessie nodded. "We're off, then," she told him.

She and Andrew hadn't gone more than a few feet along the trail when she heard Dan rushing to catch up with them.

"I'll just walk a short distance with you," he said, his face bright red from the effort.

Bessie and Andrew exchanged glances, and then Bessie set off at a rapid pace. Andrew fell in behind her, and they marched quickly along the muddy path.

"Um, Bessie," Dan called after a few minutes. "I'm going to have to turn back. My shoes are getting ruined."

Bessie looked down at Dan's feet. They were caked in mud beyond the tops of his shoes. "If you really want to start hiking the trails, I can suggest a good place to get hiking boots," she told him.

He shrugged. "I, that is, maybe another time." He turned and disappeared back the way they'd come.

Andrew put his hand on Bessie's arm. "Now can we walk a bit more slowly and maybe try to avoid the muddiest places instead of charging right through them?"

Bessie laughed. "I'm sorry, but I wanted to get rid of Dan as quickly as possible."

Andrew looked back over his shoulder. "You certainly seem to have done that."

He took her hand, and they began to stroll slowly together along the path. When Peel Castle came into view, Andrew stopped.

"It's incredibly beautiful here," he sighed. "Sometimes I want to give up my life in London and just move here."

"I can't imagine living in London."

"And I can't really imagine living anywhere else. I am coming to love the island, but I suspect London will always be home to me. I don't like being this far away from my children, anyway. I can't imagine having to fly or take a ferry every time I wanted to see them."

Bessie nodded. "The island doesn't suit everyone."

"But the views are amazing," Andrew sighed.

They walked in silence for several minutes before he spoke again.

"We were going to talk about the case."

"It's all very sad," Bessie said.

"It is. Those young people all had bright futures in front of them. I feel incredibly sorry for Julie and her family, although I'm certain her death affected the five men and women who were at the cabin with her, and their families, as well."

"I've no sympathy for whoever killed her," Bessie said flatly.

"No, and that's one of the reasons why I agreed to have the unit look at this case. Julie's killer has had fifteen more years of life than she had. I'd like to put him or her behind bars for the next fifteen or more."

Bessie nodded. "Do you have someone at the top of your list?"

He shrugged. "I'm trying to reserve judgment, but I will say that some of the suspects seemed more likeable than others in their interviews."

"Indeed. I didn't care for Harvey at all," Bessie said sharply.

"I didn't expect you would," he told her with a grin. "He comes across as a very spoiled young man."

"He seemed to me to be more upset about the inconvenience of having to speak to the police than he was about Julie's death. He kept complaining about having other things that he needed to do."

Andrew nodded. "His parents had a similar attitude when they were questioned."

"And that's where he'd learned it, of course," Bessie sighed. "I got the impression from his statement that he'd been pretty much drunk the entire weekend."

"Yes, he seemed to have done nothing but drink beer and watch movies. The women did all of the cooking, and from what he said, he didn't bother to eat much."

"The women should have made the men cook some of the meals," Bessie said.

"I quite agree, but I got the impression that, at that time, in this particular small town in America, men and women were still following more traditional gender roles."

"Yes, I got that impression as well. Many of the mothers were still stay-at-home parents."

"So you didn't care for Harvey."

"Not even a little bit. That doesn't mean I think he killed Julie, but I do think that he thought of himself as considerably more important than everyone else at the cabin."

THE CARTER FILE

"Yes, and again, his parents seemed to feel the same way. They argued that Harvey shouldn't be questioned at all as there was no way he'd had anything to do with the murder, and they insisted that his father be present in his interviews, acting as his lawyer, of course."

"Which is odd," Bessie argued.

"The police seem to have questioned him very carefully, no doubt because his father was in the room," Andrew sighed.

"They were equally careful with his parents," Bessie suggested. "And his parents had some interesting theories as to what might have happened."

"I don't think there was anyone they didn't try to blame, aside from Harvey, of course."

"They seemed particularly critical of Katie and of Mike."

"The two members of the group whose parents didn't belong to the Greenview Country Club."

"Really?"

Andrew shrugged. "That was how the detective in Pennsylvania described it to me when I mentioned the negative things that Harvey's parents had said about Katie and Mike."

"But Julie was part of their social circle," Bessie said thoughtfully.

"She was, although I don't believe that Harvey's mother approved of Julie's mother."

"But we were talking about Harvey and how much better than everyone else he thought he was," Bessie said.

"Including his girlfriend, Mary Ellen," Andrew suggested.

"Indeed. I hope she didn't end up marrying Harvey. She deserved better."

"You were more impressed with her, then?"

"She seemed shocked and upset, but also smart. She came right out and told the policeman who interviewed her that the killer had to have been one of the five people in the cabin, while Harvey kept insisting that the killer must have been an intruder who'd broken in."

"She was very forthcoming about the fact that the cabin belonged to her parents and that they'd supplied all of the alcohol. Presumably she didn't expect them to get into any trouble over the matter."

"And did they?" Bessie asked.

Andrew shook his head. "No charges were ever brought against anyone with regard to supplying alcohol to minors. When I spoke to the detective in Pennsylvania who first brought the case to my attention, he told me that those sorts of parties were common in the eighties. He claimed that they happen less frequently now, but that as long as no one is driving or making too much noise, the police have no reason to interfere."

"Except this time a woman was murdered," Bessie muttered.

"And it was the first murder in the town in thirty-six years," Andrew told her. "That previous one was the result of a fight between two drunks, and there were a half dozen witnesses who testified as to exactly what had happened."

"Have there been any murders since?" Bessie asked.

"Two, both related to illegal drugs. It's a problem everywhere, even in small-town America."

Bessie nodded. "But we were talking about Mary Ellen. She came across as one of the more intelligent of the group. I didn't feel as if she was all that fond of Harvey, though, in spite of their having been a couple for years."

"Yes, she was polite about him, but she almost seemed to be trying to distance herself from him."

"She claimed that she hadn't been drinking very much and that she and Harvey hadn't been intimate at all during the weekend," Bessie added.

"Harvey told a different story, though. He claimed he and Mary Ellen spent hours in the bedroom every day."

"In between him drinking and watching movies," Bessie said. "On balance, I believe her more than him."

"According to Harvey, there wasn't much else to do. It rained the entire weekend, and no one left the cabin."

Bessie nodded. "Mary Ellen talked about playing board games and cards. No one mentioned bringing any books."

Andrew chuckled. "Not everyone takes books everywhere they go."

"Why ever not?"

He shook his head. "I'm not certain. I always have a book in my car, and I bring several when I go on holiday. I have half a dozen in my cottage right now, even though I fully intend to visit the two bookshops on the island while I'm here."

They'd walked for some distance now, and the gentle climb began to become more challenging as the path led them up a large hill. Bessie slowed her pace even further and then stopped and turned around.

"The views are wonderful from here," she sighed. "You can see the beach and the castle."

Andrew stared for several minutes before he spoke. "I'd love to build a house right here," he said. "Then I could sit and stare at that view all day long."

After a while, they began to walk again, slowly and carefully, along the rocky path.

"Mary Ellen's parents didn't seem very cooperative," Bessie commented as they went.

"Her mother was too busy to be interviewed until two days after the murder," Andrew said. "And her father insisted on sitting in with Mary Ellen, the same as Harvey's father had done with Harvey."

"At least Mary Ellen complained about it and said she didn't need babysitting," Bessie recalled.

"But her father didn't leave, and again, I feel as if the police were very careful with what they asked her."

Bessie sighed. "I suppose we should be glad that the two lawyers didn't sit in on every interview. No one would have answered any questions."

"What did you think of Mary Ellen's mother?"

"She seemed incredibly annoyed to have to take time out of her busy schedule to talk to the police, and she managed to slip in a rude comment about Harvey's mother while complaining."

"Yes, something about not everyone having the luxury of being a stay-at-home mother to an adult who didn't need her," Andrew said with a grin. "I don't think the two women were fond of one another, even though their husbands were business partners."

"And Mary Ellen's mother wanted Mary Ellen to marry Harvey one day. She was very clear on that in her interview. She wouldn't even consider that he could have had something to do with Julie's death, calling him her future son-in-law throughout the conversation."

"Whereas Harvey's mother said she liked Mary Ellen but wanted her son to try seeing other women when he started college."

"I can't wait to find out what happened to those two," Bessie murmured.

"What about Jack Morton?" Andrew asked.

"He seemed nice, actually. Nowhere near as arrogant as Harvey, at least. He admitted to having been drunk pretty much from the time they'd arrived until the body was found, even saying that he'd been sick several times from drinking too much."

"Yes, which wasn't very smart."

"He did say that he didn't typically drink. Presumably he didn't know his limits."

"Let's hope he learned them after that weekend."

"His father seemed quite sensible. He was clearly badly shaken by the murder, though. He talked a lot about how he'd known all of the men and women since birth."

"What did you think of Jack's mother?"

"She seemed, I don't know, slightly vague, as if she wasn't entirely certain why she needed to speak to the police or what all the fuss was about. I don't feel as if she truly understood that someone had been murdered and that her son was a suspect."

Andrew nodded. "When I spoke to the detective, he told me that she'd been fighting cancer for more than a year when Julie died. Apparently she was taking a cocktail of drugs, both for treatment and for pain, which may have dulled her senses and confused her. Sadly, she passed away less than a year after the murder."

"That is sad. She still had small children, didn't she?"

"The youngest was seven when she died," Andrew said.

Bessie frowned. "What a shame."

"Anything else about Jack?" Andrew asked after a moment.

"He seemed to care a great deal about his girlfriend, Katie Dawson."

"Yes, he insisted that she couldn't possibly have had anything to do with the murder."

"And she said much the same about him. I felt as if she was rather intimidated by the others, though. She seemed almost in awe of Harvey and Mary Ellen."

"They were the wealthiest and most popular kids in the school. She was a part of the crowd only because she was involved with Jack."

"She wouldn't say anything bad about anyone in her

interview. When the police asked her who she thought had killed Julie, she insisted that it had to have been someone who'd broken into the cabin. She refused to believe that it could have been one of her friends," Bessie said. "She had to have known that she was wrong, though."

"I thought her parents had some interesting opinions."

Bessie laughed. "They were very clear about whom they suspected. It was obvious that they didn't care for Harvey or his parents. I was surprised that they flat out accused him of the murder, though."

"They both said that they felt that Harvey considered himself above the law."

"And there's probably some truth to that. Mary Ellen's parents certainly did when it came to the laws about drinking age."

Andrew nodded. "Katie's parents stated that they hadn't wanted Katie to go to the cabin in the first place, but that they'd allowed Jack to persuade them that he'd look after Katie while she was there."

"And he seems to have tried to do that, aside from when he was being sick from drinking too much."

"What about Mike? What did you think of him?"

"He seemed to think that everyone thought he was the killer," Bessie said. "I suppose he may have seemed the mostly likely suspect because it was his girlfriend who was murdered."

"And they'd had a fight," Andrew added.

"Yes, but he was pretty vague about what they'd fought about."

"Everyone was pretty vague on what Mike and Julie had fought about, even though it came up in every single interview."

"Do you think they were all lying to protect someone?"

"Maybe, or maybe they were all just too drunk to actually

THE CARTER FILE

remember what had happened," Andrew said with a sigh. "Mike said it was just a stupid disagreement over nothing, but that Julie had moved out onto the couch rather than share a bedroom with him for the last night."

"I can't help but feel that if we knew what the fight was about, we'd be closer to finding the killer."

"I agree, but the police have been trying to get an answer to that question for fifteen years without success. I can't see anyone changing his or her story now."

"Mary Ellen claimed she didn't drink much, but she also said she'd missed the fight and only found out later that it had happened. How big was the cabin?" Bessie asked.

"It had four bedrooms and three bathrooms, so more of a house than a cabin," Andrew told her. "There was a game room at the back of the house, which is where they played board games while Harvey was watching television in the living room at the front of the cabin."

"So if Julie and Mike had their fight in the living room, and Mary Ellen was in the game room, she could have missed it."

"She also might have been in a bedroom. The bedrooms were all upstairs," Andrew replied.

"Some cabin."

Andrew nodded. "I thought tonight it might be interesting to try to put together a timeline for the weekend. Maybe we can work out when Mike and Julie had their fight and where everyone else was while it was happening."

Bessie nodded. "Didn't the police do that at the time?"

"They did, and I have a copy of their timeline. I want to try to create ours based on what everyone said in the interviews, and then compare ours with the original one."

"Do you think we should turn around now?" Bessie asked. They were high in the hills over Peel, and the wind was picking up speed. Storm clouds seemed to be gathering above them, and Bessie doubted that they'd get back to Andrew's car before the rain started.

Andrew looked up at the sky and frowned. "We're going to get soaked, aren't we?" he asked as they turned around and began their hike back to the car.

CHAPTER 5

Good fortune smiled upon them, and they reached Andrew's car just moments before the skies opened and heavy rain began to fall. Bessie, sitting in the passenger seat, had to laugh as the rain crashed against her window.

"That was close," she said.

"I think we'll sit here for a bit and see if it passes," Andrew replied. "I don't want to drive in this downpour if I can avoid doing so."

Ten minutes later the rain had slowed to a lighter but steady pattern. Andrew sighed and started the car. "You were going to make pudding for tonight," he said as he began to drive out of Peel. "I hope you'll still have time to make something."

"I still have some shortbread left over from last night," Bessie told him. "We can have that with ice cream and caramel sauce. I bought the ice cream and the sauce for my guests last night and then forgot to offer it to them."

"That sounds delicious. Maybe I won't eat much dinner."

When they got back to Laxey, Andrew headed to his

cottage to check his emails and get his copy of the case file. "I have a floor plan for the cabin," he said. "I'll bring that back with me as well."

Bessie spent a few minutes tidying the cottage, even running the vacuum through the ground-floor rooms. When that was done, she carried a chair from the dining room into the kitchen and shuffled the other chairs around the table to make room for the extra one. It would be a tight fit, but she never used the dining room. The table there was covered in books, which made it difficult. Andrew arrived just moments before Hugh got there.

"Have you done all of your homework?" Bessie demanded as she let Hugh into the cottage.

"Yes, I have," he said happily. "There wasn't all that much there once I sat down to do it, and Grace gave me a biscuit for every ten minutes that I worked."

"It seems as if that would encourage you to work more slowly," Andrew suggested.

"Except I was anxious to get done so that I could play with Aalish," Hugh replied. "And once I was done, I was allowed unlimited biscuits, anyway."

Bessie laughed. "It sounds as if your lovely wife knows exactly how to encourage you."

Hugh nodded. "Aalish helps, too. She stands next to me and shouts until I stop and play with her."

"Stands? Does that mean she's walking now?" Bessie asked.

"She's starting to put a few steps together here and there, but she isn't exactly walking, not just yet," Hugh explained. "But go and see for yourself. Grace would love to see you. She mentioned that she wanted to discuss something with you, actually."

"Is anything wrong?" Bessie asked.

"I don't believe so, but there's definitely something on her mind," Hugh replied. "She told me that it wasn't anything she wanted me to worry about, but that she thought you could help."

Bessie frowned. "I'll go and see her tomorrow," she promised.

"I'll let her know to expect you. She'll be up early. Aalish is now waking up around six every morning, and we can't seem to get her to sleep any later."

"Six is a perfectly good time to get up in the morning," Bessie argued.

Hugh made a face. "I prefer seven, but I won't complain, as Aalish is going to bed nicely around eight each evening, which gives Grace and me at least an hour together before one of us falls asleep in the middle of a sentence."

Bessie laughed and then opened the door to another knock. John and Doona walked in, carrying several large boxes.

"Pizza?" Bessie asked.

"The restaurant across from the station is now a different pizza place," Doona told her. "They do a variety of what they're calling artisan pizzas, with rather unusual toppings."

"Unusual toppings?" Bessie repeated.

"Rosemary chicken with fennel and asparagus," Doona told her.

"On a pizza?" Bessie asked.

"Oh, yes. They also had eggplant, mushroom, onions, and peppers," Doona replied.

"What did you get?" Bessie asked apprehensively.

"The woman behind the counter was most disappointed in me when I asked for two with plain cheese and one with just onions and peppers," Doona told her. "The cheese ones do have about half a dozen different cheeses on them, but I doubt I'll be able to taste them all."

She put the pizza boxes on the counter while Bessie got down plates for everyone.

"There's garlic bread, too," John said. "It's some sort of specialty bread with butter, garlic, parsley, and herbs."

Bessie smiled at the crusty loaf of bread that John pulled out of a bag. "That looks delicious," she said.

Everyone filled plates, and then the group chatted about the case while they ate. It seemed that they all shared Bessie's dislike of Harvey, but no one was willing to suggest who they thought had killed Julie.

"I thought that after dinner we could try to work out a timeline for the entire weekend," Andrew told them. "I'm not certain it will help, but it can't hurt. I have the original timeline that the police created right after the murder. It might be interesting to compare ours with theirs once we're done."

Doona cleared away the dinner plates while Bessie put slices of shortbread into bowls. She topped each slice with a generous scoop of vanilla ice cream and then added a large dollop of caramel sauce. John did the washing-up after everyone had finished eating pudding.

Bessie made tea and put the rest of the shortbread out on a plate for them to enjoy while they talked. Andrew pulled out a notebook and a pen.

"Graduation was at seven o'clock in the evening," he said, making a note. "The ceremony lasted about an hour, and then apparently some time was spent taking photographs and whatnot. Harvey and Mary Ellen were the first to head to the cabin."

Bessie flipped through her notes. "They went together in Harvey's car," she said. "Mary Ellen thought they'd arrived around nine. Harvey said he wasn't paying any attention to the time."

"And according to his statement, he started drinking

before he'd even brought the suitcases into the cabin," Doona added.

"Mary Ellen said that she actually went out and got her own suitcase, as Harvey was too busy drinking to bother. She didn't get his, though, so he had to go back out a short while later, by which time the rain had started," John said, looking up from his notes. "The other two couples arrived in the rain."

"Mike and Julie were next," Bessie read from her notes. "They came in Julie's car. It had been a graduation present from her parents, a little red convertible that nearly got stuck in the mud on the way to the cabin."

"It left quite distinct tyre tracks along the muddy road that led to the cabin," Andrew said. "Mike reckoned they arrived at the cabin not long before ten. He said he wasn't really paying attention to the time, but that he'd spent about half an hour with his family after the graduation ceremony before Julie collected him to take him to the cabin."

"And then, about half an hour later, Jack and Katie arrived," Doona interjected. "Jack and his family had gone out for dinner after the ceremony."

"And Katie wasn't invited," Bessie said thoughtfully.

"But as soon as dinner was over, he collected her and took her to the cabin," Hugh said. "He was driving a truck that was one of the four vehicles that the family owned. His mother made some comment about him not necessarily having permission to take the truck, but then she backtracked when the police tried to question her further."

"So by ten o'clock, all six people were at the cabin," Bessie said. "And from all accounts, they were all drinking."

"They had quite a selection of options," John said. "Wine, beer, vodka, rum, and wine coolers, whatever those are."

"A mixture of wine and fruit juice with fizzy water and sugar," Andrew told him. "I asked the detective to explain them to me. He said that they were popular in the eighties, and have more or less disappeared in the years since."

"That was what the women were drinking, for the most part," Bessie recalled. "Mary Ellen said that her parents had told her that they shouldn't drink any of the rum or vodka."

"Except Harvey had a few shots of rum when he first arrived," Doona remembered. "He mentioned it in his interview and sounded quite proud of himself, really."

"He seemed to think that the rules didn't apply to him," Hugh said.

"And considering how Mary Ellen's mother felt about him, he may have been right, at least about drinking the rum," John added.

"So we have the six young people getting drunk almost immediately," Andrew said. "They put a movie in the VCR and popped some popcorn. Jack and Katie were the first to head to bed, not long after midnight, according to Katie's statement."

"She had a part-time job, and she'd had to work that morning," Bessie recalled, searching her notes. "She'd been up since six, and she said that by midnight she was falling asleep in front of the movie, so she decided to go to bed."

"And Jack went with her," Hugh added.

"And they went straight to sleep, according to both of them," Doona said.

"Mike and Julie headed up to their bedroom as soon as the movie finished," Hugh said. "Mike told the police that Harvey tried to persuade him to stay up and drink more, but that he was tired and he wanted some time alone with Julie. Apparently they rarely got to spend much time alone together, at least not in a situation where they could, well, be intimate."

"Which is what he claims happened when they went

upstairs," Doona said. "We don't have her statement to compare with his, of course."

"That left just Harvey and Mary Ellen in the living room," Bessie said. "Mary Ellen said that she headed to bed not long after, but that she left Harvey on his own, still drinking."

"And that's the first inconsistency between their statements," Hugh pointed out. "He claims that they went up to bed together about an hour after the others."

Andrew nodded. "Whoever was telling the truth, they both agreed that no one got up before midday the next day."

"Mary Ellen said that she was the first one up and that she went down and started making breakfast for everyone," Bessie recalled, checking her notes. "She said she wasn't much of a cook, but she could scramble eggs and fry bacon. She also said she started a pot of coffee."

"And then Julie and Mike came down," Hugh said, reading from his notes. "Julie helped with breakfast while Mike drank coffee."

"Mary Ellen said that all three of them were drinking coffee. So much so that she had to start a second pot before anyone else came down," John added.

"And Jack and Katie came down while the second pot was still brewing," Doona said. "That just left Harvey tucked up in bed."

"But he came down as Mary Ellen started serving breakfast," Bessie said. "She claimed she called up to him, telling him to come down, but he said that he woke up on his own and went down when he smelled bacon and coffee."

"That would get me out of bed," Doona said.

"Me too," Hugh agreed.

"So they ate breakfast and then, by all accounts, they started drinking," John said.

"Mary Ellen said that they had planned to walk in the

woods and spend time on the beach. The cabin was on a small lake, after all. Unfortunately, it was still raining heavily, and it was quite cold for June, as well," Bessie read from her notes.

"So they started drinking and playing cards," Doona said. "Everyone went into the game room at the back of the cabin to play games, except for Harvey, who put a movie on the television."

"VCRs were still pretty new in those days, weren't they?" Bessie asked, trying to remember.

"They certainly weren't common at that point," Andrew told her. "But this was the vacation home of a wealthy family. They had a collection of videos to go with the player. Harvey's family had one too, but it seemed that their video collection didn't include the sorts of movies he enjoyed."

"What sorts of movies?" Bessie wondered.

Andrew shrugged. "Harvey listed every movie that he watched that weekend in this statement. Most of them seemed to be movies with car chases and lots of explosions."

"And he preferred watching them to spending time with his friends," Bessie said in a disapproving tone.

"Apparently, anyway," Andrew replied.

"From what I read, that was pretty much how they spent the entire day," Bessie said. "Around six, Mary Ellen made dinner."

"Spaghetti," Hugh recalled. "She said she just dumped some jars of sauce into a pan and heated that and then boiled some pasta."

"And they had some sort of frozen garlic bread," Doona added.

"And wine," Bessie interjected. "Mary Ellen said they opened two bottles of red wine, as that was what you drank with pasta."

"And everyone had some except for Harvey," Hugh remembered. "He kept drinking beer."

"They had a cake for pudding," Doona said. "Julie had brought it. Her mother had ordered it from the local bakery. It was a big congratulations cake for them all."

"Harvey seemed to think that it was a stupid thing for Julie to have done," Hugh added. "He was quite scornful of her effort."

"But he ate some," John added. "They all ate some from what I read."

"And then they drank more," Bessie sighed. "Most of them went back into the game room, but Harvey went back to his movies. This is where things get confused, though."

"Because of the fight between Mike and Julie," John said. "No one admitted to witnessing the fight, although they probably all did."

"Harvey said the fight took place in the game room, but everyone else said that Julie and Mike left the game room together around nine o'clock," Bessie said, looking at her notes. "Mike claims he wasn't paying attention to the time, but he agreed that he and Julie left the room together."

"And then had a huge argument," Hugh said.

"Mike claimed it was a small disagreement," Bessie countered.

"But it was bad enough that Julie went and got her things and moved herself down to the living room," Bessie pointed out.

"Where Harvey was still watching movies," Doona added.

"And then, according to Harvey, he went up to bed. He said he didn't want to get into the middle of the fight between Mike and Julie," Bessie read from her notes.

"Mary Ellen, Jack, and Katie were still in the game room. All of their statements were in agreement that they all went upstairs around ten o'clock. Mike claimed that he'd followed Julie up to their room and tried to convince her to stay with him, but that she wouldn't listen. He said that he stayed in their bedroom after she went down to the living room," Andrew said.

"Except Harvey insisted that Mike came down to try to talk to Julie, which was one reason why he headed up to bed when he did," Hugh added.

"So we have four of the six people in their rooms, Julie on the couch, and Mike either in his room or downstairs with Julie," Bessie sighed. "At some point, of course, Mike went upstairs. The question is, was Julie still alive when he went?"

"Unless he truly never did go back downstairs after the fight," Doona said. "If he didn't, then we have to wonder if Julie was still alive when Harvey went up to bed."

"The answer to that question is yes," Andrew told her. "Assuming Harvey was telling the truth about when he went to bed, at least. The coroner reckoned that Julie died around three o'clock in the morning, certainly no earlier."

"And any one of the five could have gone down and killed her," John said. "No one admitted to going back downstairs after midnight, but they wouldn't, would they?"

"Would one of them have noticed if his or her partner had disappeared in the night for some length of time?" Bessie wondered.

"I suppose that depends on how deeply asleep they all were. We know they'd been drinking. Some of them may have been closer to passed out than asleep," Andrew suggested.

Bessie frowned. "Mary Ellen claimed that she hadn't had that much to drink. She also claimed that she would have noticed if Harvey had left the room for more than a minute or two."

"And he said the same about her," John added. "Thus providing alibis for one another."

"Katie and Jack did much the same thing, although Katie

was more uncertain about whether she would have noticed if Jack had left the room or not," Doona said.

"Most of them seemed to be trying to be very careful with what they said," Bessie added. "I felt as if they were doing everything they could to not point fingers at Mike, even as they tried to alibi themselves."

Andrew nodded. "Because, of course, there was no one to alibi Mike. He was sleeping alone after his fight with Julie."

"And no one seems to know what they fought about," Bessie sighed.

"What if they fought about one of the other women?" Hugh asked. "Or one of the other men? What I mean is, what if one of them was secretly involved with one of the others, and then the other person found out?"

"I think you lost me with all those others," Doona laughed. "But I know what you mean. Maybe Julie was seeing Harvey behind Mike's back, and Mike found out."

"Or any other combination of people," Andrew said. "But if that were the case, why were only Julie and Mike fighting? Surely if one of them was seeing one of the others and it became common knowledge, there would have been two couples arguing that evening."

"I think the police in Pennsylvania need to interview Mike again," Bessie said. "They need to find out exactly what he and Julie fought about."

"He was vague fifteen years ago," Andrew told her. "I can't imagine he's going to be any less so today, but I'll ask them to try."

"Of course, we don't know what's happened to everyone yet," John said. "We'll probably have very different questions for them all once we find out what they've done over the past fifteen years."

"And that's a conversation for tomorrow," Andrew said with a smile.

CHAPTER 6

The group talked for a while longer about their timeline, but they didn't reach any conclusions. Andrew compared their version with the original police timeline and found no major differences.

"We'll start tomorrow by discussing how likely we think each of the suspects is as the murderer," Andrew told them as they all began to gather up their paperwork. "And then I'll give you a brief update as to where they all are now. The police recently interviewed them all again. I have those complete statements for you."

"Tell Grace I'll see her tomorrow," Bessie reminded Hugh as she let him out.

He nodded and gave her a hug. "Thanks," he replied.

John and Doona were right behind him.

"We'll see you at two tomorrow," John said, giving Bessie a hug. She hugged him and then Doona and then let them out.

"I hope you aren't too cross that I haven't shared the recent updates yet," Andrew said to Bessie as she walked back to the kitchen table.

"It's frustrating, but I do understand. I know I'd have rushed to read them, and then that information would have coloured my opinions on the suspects."

He nodded. "To be honest, I haven't read them myself yet. I'm going to read them in the morning and take a few notes so that I can give you all the basics at the meeting tomorrow. Would you like to have lunch with me at the Seaview before the meeting?"

"Yes, please," Bessie replied. That would leave her morning free to talk with Grace and find out what was bothering the girl. Hugh hadn't seemed too worried, so she told herself it wasn't anything important, but it was difficult for her to not be concerned. She thought the world of Grace, who was pretty, smart, and perfect for Hugh.

She and Andrew talked about the case for a few minutes longer, but they both found themselves yawning between sentences after a short while.

"I think we both need an early night," Bessie laughed in between yawns.

"You may be right," Andrew agreed. "I'm telling you, it's the sea air. It helps me sleep more than any tablets I've ever taken."

"I've been breathing the sea air for decades," Bessie replied. "I never have trouble sleeping, but I'm not usually this tired this early in the evening."

"Perhaps we've been thinking too much. Maybe our brains need a rest."

"I'm not going to argue," Bessie said around another yawn.

She let Andrew out and watched him walk to his cottage. When he was safely inside and she saw a light go on in the cottage's sitting room, she shut and locked her door. It took her only a moment to tidy the kitchen. Grabbing the book she'd been reading, she headed up to bed, expecting that she'd read a few chapters before she felt asleep.

Once she was in her pyjamas, under the duvet, though, she found that she couldn't keep her eyes open. *The book is good, but clearly not good enough,* she thought as she slid a bookmark into place and then set the book on her bedside table. Wondering if she'd wake up extra early, Bessie switched off the light and fell asleep almost immediately.

IT WAS quarter past six when Bessie woke up the next morning, somewhat later than usual. Hoping she wasn't brewing something, she got out of bed and got herself ready for the day. Not wanting to turn up at Grace's house too early, she made herself breakfast before she headed out for her walk. The holiday cottages were all dark as she walked past them. Clearly, Andrew was still in bed. As she walked along, a light suddenly went on in one of the bedrooms in one of the cottages.

Bessie stopped and waited to see what would happen next. A few minutes later, a light was turned on in the sitting room of the cottage. Sighing with relief, Bessie waved to Pat, the young man who was helping Thomas and Maggie get the cottages ready for spring. He waved back and then walked over to the sliding doors and slid them open.

"Good morning, Bessie," he called.

Bessie crossed the beach to him, pleased to see that he was looking happier and healthier than he had when they'd first met. "Good morning," she replied. "How's the painting coming?"

Pat made a face. "I suppose I'm getting better at it, but I'm still not enjoying it," he told her. "I mean, it's a job, and I'm hugely grateful to Thomas and Maggie for giving me a job and a place to stay, but I'm learning very quickly that I'd rather do just about anything than paint walls."

"Have you tried painting ceilings yet?"

Pat laughed. "Yes, okay, you're right. Ceilings are worse. Luckily, they're having me paint the ceilings only when we absolutely have to. So far I've only had to do a few."

"I'm sure Thomas and Maggie are happy to have you."

Thomas had been unwell for over a year, and Bessie knew that there was no way Maggie had the time or the energy to paint all of the cottages herself during the winter months. A month earlier, Pat had been homeless and breaking into one of the cottages in order to have a place to stay. Bessie was pleased that his arrangement with Thomas and Maggie seemed to be working for all of them.

"They seem happy enough with my work, too, even though I'm not a very good painter," Pat laughed. "Maggie keeps bringing me food, like proper hot meals and then puddings. I've had more cake in the past fortnight than I'd had in the last ten years."

"Maggie likes to have people to fuss over," Bessie told him. "I suspect Thomas is quite tired of her fussing over him."

"He's a good guy. I hope he's going to be okay. Sometimes he seems to be doing better, but then other days he looks really unwell."

Bessie nodded. "I think he and Maggie should go somewhere warm for a holiday, but they don't want to leave the cottages unattended."

"They aren't unattended, though. I'm here now," Pat said. "I'm going to have to talk to Maggie and suggest that they go away. I can keep an eye on things here for a fortnight or so."

"If I see her, I'll suggest the same thing," Bessie told him. "Andrew is their only guest at the moment, and he's only staying for a few weeks each month."

Pat nodded and then looked down at the ground. "I never did thank you properly, really," he muttered. "Thanks."

"You're welcome," Bessie told him. "I'm glad I could help."

"You've changed my life," Pat countered. "Maggie's talked me into going back to school. I'm going to start working on a few GCSEs. If I can get those, I may even stay in school and work towards, well, I don't know what."

Bessie laughed. "I admire your enthusiasm," she told him. "It sounds as if anything would be better than painting, anyway."

"Painting isn't that bad, really. I shouldn't complain."

As Pat headed back inside to get ready for his day, Bessie continued down the beach. When she reached the stairs to Thie yn Traie, she glanced up at them. She still hadn't heard anything certain about when the Quayles would be back on the island. Perhaps she'd wait a few days and then try ringing the house to see if anyone was at home. Bessie missed her friend, Mary, and was eager to see her again.

The walk from there to the new houses seemed to take longer than normal. Bessie was feeling quite tired by the time the houses came into view. If Grace's plans had changed and she wasn't at home, the walk back to Treoghe Bwaane was going to be a very long one. Hoping to find her friend ready to welcome her with tea and a comfortable chair, Bessie walked a bit faster towards the home that belonged to Hugh and Grace.

The houses in the row were quite close together. They were fairly large, and Bessie knew that they'd been quite expensive when they'd first been put on the market. A detached house with four bedrooms right on the beach was outside of the budget for Hugh and Grace, but they'd been able to get a considerable discount on the property because a man had been murdered in the house's dining room. Bessie thought about that as she crossed the sand.

While Grace had been worried about living with the house's unfortunate history, the house now felt as if it was a much-loved family home, at least to Bessie. The little family had plenty of room to grow, and the location was just about ideal. As Bessie approached the sliding doors at the back of the property, she spotted Aalish crawling in circles around Grace, who was sitting in the middle of the floor. When she reached the doors, Bessie tapped lightly.

Grace looked up and then said something to Aalish. The baby looked over at Bessie and burst into tears. Grace flushed and then got to her feet.

"I do apologise for my daughter," she said as she pulled the door open. "She's in a bit of a mood this morning."

Aalish was still crawling around the room, more whimpering than crying. She seemed to be ignoring both Bessie and her mother.

"She doesn't want visitors this morning," Bessie guessed as she walked into the house.

"Or one of a million other things," Grace sighed. "Sometimes I feel as if I'm actually starting to understand her, and other times she's a complete mystery to me."

"I believe that's perfectly normal."

Grace shrugged. "It's still annoying."

"But how are you?" Bessie asked. "Hugh said you wanted to speak with me about something."

Grace frowned. "I do, or rather, I think I do, but it's probably nothing."

"What's probably nothing?"

"But where are my manners? Come in and have a seat," Grace said. "Let me put the kettle on. It's cold out there. I'm sure you'd love a cuppa and a few biscuits."

Bessie couldn't argue with that, and she wasn't really in any hurry to hear what Grace wanted, either. She took a seat at the kitchen island, happy to get off of her feet for a short while. Aalish crawled past her, now babbling to herself quite contentedly.

"She's growing up quickly," Bessie remarked.

Grace looked at Aalish and frowned. "Too quickly. I don't want to keep her a baby forever, but I think I'd quite enjoy a few more months at this stage before she rushes into the next one. I don't get a choice, though. She's already doing everything she can to learn to walk and climb and drive a car and leave home."

Bessie raised an eyebrow.

Grace laughed. "I may be exaggerating slightly," she admitted as she put biscuits onto a plate. "Aalish? Do you want a biscuit?" she asked, holding up a plain digestive.

Aalish was halfway across the room. She stopped and stared at her mother for a moment and then crawled as quickly as she could towards her, shouting random sounds that made Bessie laugh.

"I take it that's a yes," Bessie said as Aalish stopped at her mother's feet and moved into a sitting position, still shouting.

"One we can both understand," Grace laughed. She picked up the baby and handed her the biscuit.

A moment later, the kettle boiled. Grace set Aalish back on the floor with her biscuit while she made tea. Bessie watched as the girl gnawed on the sweet treat, her eyes on her mother the entire time. As Grace handed Bessie a teacup, Aalish began to shout again. When Grace looked over at her, Aalish tossed what was left of her biscuit into the air. The half-eaten biscuit went up a short distance and then came back down, bouncing off of Aalish's head on its way to the ground.

Aalish looked shocked for a moment and then began to shout. Grace muttered something under her breath as she picked up the biscuit and put it in the bin. Then she scooped up Aalish and held her close.

"Did that big bad biscuit attack you?" she asked. "You poor, poor thing. Mummy needs to work harder to keep you safe from dangerous foods."

Bessie reached for the plate in front of her. As she brought a biscuit up to her lips, she made eye contact with Aalish. The baby stared hard at Bessie and then shrieked her disapproval.

"I don't think she wants anyone to have biscuits now," Bessie said, quickly putting hers down on the small plate in front of her.

"More like she wants your biscuit," Grace replied. She picked up a biscuit from the plate and held it out to Aalish. The girl grabbed it eagerly and shoved it in her mouth.

"You'll choke yourself if you aren't careful," Grace warned. Balancing the baby on her hip, she picked up a biscuit of her own.

Bessie took a sip of tea. "Now that we're all happy, what did you want to discuss with me?" she asked.

Grace flushed. "It's probably nothing," she said.

"Then you should be happy to tell me all about it."

"One of my friends is missing," Grace blurted out.

"That sounds as if it should be a job for the police. You should talk to Hugh and probably John."

Grace shook her head. "It isn't a police matter. She's not really missing, not in the traditional sense. She's just, well, I'm not sure how to describe it, taking a break, maybe."

"I'm confused," Bessie admitted.

"I'm going to have to tell you the whole story," Grace sighed. "My friend is called Erica, Erica Tucker. She's twenty-five and she's single. We worked together a few years ago. She used to be a teacher, but she got tired of children and went to work for a bank instead."

"Tired of children?" Bessie asked, amused.

"I think she may have been more tired of the parents than the children, but whatever, she took a job in the lending department of one of the local banks and was really happy to be doing something different."

"And then what happened?" Bessie asked after a long pause.

"Oh, she worked for the local bank for about a year and then took a job in Liverpool with one of the biggest banks in the country. She moved across and bought herself a flat for a lot less than a flat here would have cost. She's been in Liverpool ever since."

"Except now she's missing?"

"I don't know. We don't talk all that often, maybe once or twice a month. I'll send her a text just to say hello, or she'll email me to let me know how she's doing. She was home for a week in October, and she came over and met Aalish. We both promised that we'd do better about keeping in touch, but you know how that goes."

Bessie nodded. "You both had good intentions."

"We did and, for a few weeks, we were texting back and forth almost regularly. I made a point of texting her every Sunday afternoon, just to say hello. She usually texted back with a story or two about her weekend. She's been out with a lot of different men since she's been in Liverpool, and she loves telling me stories about them all."

Aalish put the last of her biscuit into the mouth and immediately began to wiggle and twist in her mother's arms.

"Let's clean up your hands and face before I put you down," Grace told her.

Bessie thought it was a perfectly reasonable request. Aalish was practically covered in soggy, crushed biscuit pieces. Of course, Aalish didn't agree. As soon as Grace moved towards the sink, she began to scream and fight to get away. Grace held her hands under the running water while Aalish sobbed. Then Grace ran a wet paper towel over her daughter's face. The crying continued while Grace tried to dry Aalish's hands and arms.

"The poor child," Bessie laughed as Grace put the still crying baby on the floor.

Grace sighed as Aalish stopped crying and crawled over to a pile of toys in the corner. She was babbling happily to a cuddly dog a moment later. "She could convince anyone that I'm torturing her," Grace said.

"She was probably planning to eat the crumbs later. But you were telling me about Erica."

"The last two times I've texted her, she hasn't replied," Grace said. She looked at Bessie and flushed. "It sounds silly when I say that. She might just be really busy, or maybe she's ignoring me for some reason."

"How long has it been since you heard from her?"

"Three weeks," Grace said. "But that isn't unusual. As I said before, after we saw each other, we said we'd keep in touch more often, but that didn't last long. I texted every Sunday for a few weeks, and then I missed one or two. Erica never complains and, if I go too long between texts, she'll send one to me."

"But now she hasn't been replying?"

"I texted her three days ago, just to say hello, and she didn't reply. Sometimes it takes her half a day or even a full day to get back to me, but I still haven't heard back. I sent her a second text yesterday, just in case she missed the first one."

"I don't understand why you don't want to involve the police."

"Because there may be a dozen different reasons why she hasn't replied. She may even be upset with me about something, but it seems more likely she's just busy. I tried ringing her this morning, but I got her voicemail. I thought about ringing the bank and asking to speak to her, but I'm afraid they'll think she's getting personal calls at work. I don't want to get her into trouble."

"Surely, even if she's busy, she should be able to find the time to reply to your text," Bessie said thoughtfully.

"The last time this happened, she'd gone away with a new boyfriend," Grace said quietly. "I kept ringing and texting while they were, um, cuddling up together all weekend long. She may be simply ignoring her phone, but I'm slightly concerned. The last thing I want to do is start a police investigation, though. She'd never forgive me if she's just having a romantic getaway with someone."

"I'm not certain what you want me to do," Bessie said after a moment.

"I thought maybe you could suggest ways for me to find her without involving the police or embarrassing her. Something that doesn't involve me going over to Liverpool, obviously."

Bessie frowned. "I would have thought Hugh would be a better resource for that sort of thing."

"He'll want me to file a missing person report," Grace told her. "I may do so eventually, but I'm not ready yet."

"Does she have any family on the island?"

"Her mother is in a care home in Douglas, but she has problems with her memory. I thought about ringing her, but I don't want to upset her."

Bessie nodded. "I suppose I could ring the bank and ask to speak to her. Did you say she works in lending?"

"Yes, she's an assistant vice president, but I don't think the title means much."

Bessie laughed. "I could pretend that I'm interested in buying a property in Liverpool, I suppose."

"Would you?"

Grace wrote down the name of the bank and its telephone number. "They aren't open on a Sunday, of course," she said as she handed the sheet to Bessie.

"I'll ring them tomorrow morning," Bessie promised. "And then I'll let you know what I discover."

They chatted for a bit longer about nothing much before Bessie decided that she needed to get home. Grace held the sliding door open for her, catching Aalish as the girl tried to get out onto the beach.

"Thank you," Grace said. "I feel better already."

"I haven't done anything yet."

"No, but you're going to ring tomorrow and probably talk to Erica, and everything will be fine."

Bessie gave her a hug, hoping that Grace was right. Aalish waved as Grace shut the door, and Bessie began to head for home. The wind was picking up, and it felt as if it might rain at any moment as Bessie hurried across the sand. She barely noticed when she reached the stairs to Thie yn Traie. As she rushed past them, though, a voice above her called her name.

CHAPTER 7

"Bessie…" the word floated down the beach, causing Bessie to stop in her tracks.

"Elizabeth," she said, turning around and greeting with a hug the pretty young blonde who'd raced down the steps. "It's so good to see you."

"It's good to see you, too," Elizabeth replied. "I feel as if we were gone forever."

"It certainly seems to have been a long time. But you're back now. How are you? How are your parents?"

Elizabeth frowned. "I'm fine, that is, I'm mostly fine, although, well, but we can talk about that later. My father is happy to be back, but, well…" She stopped and stared at the ground.

"What's wrong?" Bessie asked.

Sighing, Elizabeth looked up at her and then back down. "Mum hasn't been well. We weren't planning to be away as long as we were, but Mum fell ill, and Dad insisted on finding her the best possible place for her treatment and recuperation. It was only when Mum was well enough to start asking to come home that he finally agreed that we should come back here."

"I'm so sorry to hear that," Bessie said, suddenly worried about her friend.

"Mum wants to see you, but travelling took a lot out of her. I wanted to let you know that she isn't ignoring you, but she's going to need a few more days before she's going to be up to having guests."

"Please tell her that I'll be thinking of her and that she's not to worry about seeing me until she's certain she's well enough."

Elizabeth nodded. "Dad's been badly shaken by everything that's happened. He doesn't want to leave Mum's side, which is sweet, but I think it's starting to annoy her. Actually, I'm certain it's starting to annoy her, but not enough for her to tell him yet."

"Now that you're back on the island, he'll start to get busy with business concerns, won't he?"

"Maybe, although he seems quite content to let my brothers deal with the business now. They come over every evening to discuss things with him, but he doesn't really listen to them. I keep hoping that once Mum is clearly doing better, he'll get back to normal."

"This all must be very difficult for you," Bessie suggested.

"It isn't easy, but I'm coping. Coming back has been harder than I'd expected, though. Things changed quite a lot while I was away."

Bessie wasn't certain how to reply to that. Elizabeth could have been referring to the two new party-planning businesses, to Andy's engagement, or to both things. It was possible, however, that Elizabeth had heard only about one or the other, and Bessie didn't want to be the bearer of bad news. "Have they?" she finally murmured.

Elizabeth stared at her for a moment and then sighed.

"I'm certain you know all about my two competitors. One of them has already given up and gone back to doing something else, but Jennifer Johnson is going to be a problem. It's only just possible that the island's population can support two party planners, but that would work only if Jennifer and I cooperated to some extent. I can't see that happening, so I'm going to have to put her out of business."

Bessie could hear determination in Elizabeth's voice that was new and sounded formidable. "That might not be easy," she warned.

"I've already spoken to a few people and learned some things about her rather questionable business practices. The island is too small, and people here talk to one another too much. You can't book the same party for multiple locations and then play them off of one another to get a better price — not more than once or twice, anyway. She may have quite a few customers, but she's soon going to find it difficult to find venues for her events if she keeps treating the island's businesses that way."

"I wish you luck," Bessie said slowly, wondering if she dared mention Andy.

"Of course, Jennifer also has a considerable asset with which I can't compete," Elizabeth admitted. "Everyone on the island wants Andy catering their events, and I don't blame them. But Andy isn't the only person in the world who can cater events. The pair of them are about to find out what competition is all about."

The look on Elizabeth's face was pure steel. *She has more of her mother in her than I'd realised,* Bessie thought. While George was a boisterous and successful businessman, and Mary was quiet and preferred to stay at home, Bessie had learned over the years that Mary was the stronger of the two and the force that had propelled George to success.

"You've heard that he's working with her, then," Bessie said.

"Oh, the answering machine was full of that message, and the news that they're engaged, as well," Elizabeth said darkly. "People love to share bad news, don't they? I wish them well personally, but professionally? I'm going to do everything I can to shut them down."

"I won't be taking sides," Bessie warned her. "Andy is still a dear friend of mine."

"Just promise me you won't get Jennifer to plan any events for you."

Bessie laughed. "You've nothing to worry about there. I can't imagine that I'll need any events planned in the foreseeable future, but if I do, I'll have you plan them."

"Thank you. That means a lot to me. Now I just have to convince the rest of the island to feel the same way."

"Do you know what you'll do for catering?" Bessie asked.

"For the moment, I'll be focussing on planning events at locations with their own catering team. The Seaview, primarily, as Jennifer is no longer welcome to hold events there, and it's still the island's premiere event location."

"Their chef is amazing," Bessie said.

"He is, and he's quite bored this time of year. There aren't many guests at the hotel, and there haven't been many special events, either. I've been speaking with him and with Jasper Coventry about having the chef do some outside catering for me. They're discussing the matter now, but you mustn't tell anyone."

"You know I won't say a word to anyone."

Elizabeth nodded. "I really don't have any quarrel with Andy, although I did feel a bit badly done to when I found out he and Jennifer were engaged. Whenever I tried to talk about marriage, he told me that we hadn't known one another long enough to discuss it. As far as I know, he's known Jennifer for six months or less."

Bessie swallowed a dozen replies. Whatever she thought of Jennifer, she needed to be carefully neutral. The woman was going to marry Andy, after all. "He has to make his own decisions," she said eventually.

"Which means you think he's making a mistake, but you're too polite to say it," Elizabeth suggested.

"I never said that," Bessie replied with a grin.

Elizabeth laughed. "Have you met her?"

"She and Andy came for dinner a few nights ago."

"What did you think of her?"

"We barely spoke, really," Bessie demurred.

"Over dinner at your cottage? People always pour out their life stories to you, given the chance. Interesting."

"Andy was there as well. We were busy catching up."

"If you say so."

"You haven't met her yet, then?"

"No, and I'm not likely to do so. I won't be going to any party she's planned. I've already made that clear to everyone I know."

A loud ringing noise interrupted the conversation. Elizabeth pulled her mobile out of her pocket and frowned at it.

"Hello?"

"Yes, I'll be right there."

"Mum needs me," she told Bessie as she dropped the device back into her pocket. "Dad's making her crazy, I suspect."

Bessie gave the girl a tight hug. "Take care of yourself. You know where I am if you need to talk."

"Thank you. I may take you up on that sooner rather than later," Elizabeth told her before she dashed away, rushing up the rickety stairs that twisted and turned on their way up the side of the cliff.

Sighing, Bessie continued on her way across the sand. A glance at her watch showed her that the day was rapidly getting away from her. Andrew would be arriving at her cottage soon, wanting to go for lunch, and she hadn't done anything useful with her day yet.

That wasn't strictly true, she told herself as she unlocked her cottage door. Her conversations with Pat, Grace, and Elizabeth had all been useful in their own way. What she hadn't done was any more work on the diaries that Marjorie Stevens from the Manx Museum Library had given her. *Surely, Carree's infatuation with the apprentice blacksmith has to be coming to an end,* she thought as she climbed the stairs to the small room she used as an office.

For many years Bessie had worked as an amateur historian, studying various documents in the museum library. After focussing on wills for years, she'd taken a class in reading old handwriting that had helped prepare her to transcribe a series of diaries from a young woman called Onnee who had moved to America after growing up on the island. Onnee's handwriting had been a struggle to read, but this second set of diaries that Marjorie had given her was a different sort of challenge.

Young Carree, worried that her younger sister would discover her secrets, had written her diaries in code. The first few entries had been written using a simple substitution code, one that had been cracked by one of the researchers on the museum staff before the diaries had been given to Bessie.

Bessie had worked her way through the first several pages, deciphering a word at a time, learning all about the girl's obsession with Harold Hartner. The last entry that she'd worked through, though, had apparently used a different code. It hadn't taken Bessie long to realise that the key that she'd been given was no longer working, but she hadn't had time to try to break the new code that day. Now she was determined to solve it and transcribe the next entry before Andrew arrived for lunch.

When he knocked on her door an hour later, Bessie was ready to go.

"How was your morning?" he asked as she followed him to his car.

"Good, I suppose."

"You aren't certain?"

"I went for a long walk and spoke to three different people. That filled a large portion of the morning. Once I was home, I worked on transcribing more of Carree's diaries."

"Ah, yes, you told me about Carree and her diaries. I believe she was still chasing after the apprentice blacksmith the last time we spoke and still writing everything in code."

"And she's still writing in code, although in a different code, which made my job a bit more difficult."

"If you're stuck, I used to be quite good at codes and ciphers."

"I'm not stuck yet, although she is trying to make things more difficult. I don't know if her sister worked out the first code or if she's simply taking precautions, but the first code was a simple case of her substituting one letter for another. This one was a bit more complex, although not terribly."

"And you've cracked it?"

"I have, only to discover that she'd finally had an opportunity to speak to Harold Hartner and, when she'd done so, she'd found him less than appealing."

Andrew laughed. "People often are when you speak to them," he suggested.

Bessie nodded. "From afar, he seemed perfect, but when they spoke she found him to be poorly educated and somewhat dull."

"Has she found someone else to transfer her affections to yet?"

"Not yet, but I don't think it will take her long."

"She does get married one day, doesn't she?"

"She does, and she eventually has two daughters, as well. I know what her surname was when she passed away, but I don't know how many times she may have been married."

"It all sounds fascinating."

"It is, rather. I just hope she doesn't keep changing the code she's using." Bessie thought for a minute and then shook her head. "Actually, I quite enjoyed the challenge of cracking her code. I just hope she doesn't change it too often, or it will take me longer to get through the diaries than it actually took her to live through the events in them."

While they'd been chatting, Andrew had driven them into Ramsey. He parked in the large car park for the Seaview and offered Bessie his arm as she emerged from the car. As they walked towards the entrance, Bessie spotted Jasper walking out of a door in the side of the building. She waved, causing him to stop and then turn and head their way.

"Hello," he said brightly. "I wasn't expecting you here much before two. I didn't get the time for the meeting wrong, did I?"

"We thought we'd have lunch in the restaurant before the meeting," Andrew explained.

"Very good," Jasper replied. "I've a small errand to run, but if you don't mind, I'll find you in the dining room when I get back. I'd appreciate Bessie's opinion on something."

"My opinion?" Bessie asked.

"I shouldn't be long," Jasper told her. "In the meantime, get the chicken option from the specials for today. It's incredible. I'm trying to convince the chef to add it to the proper menu, but you know he never does what I want him to do."

Bessie laughed. Whenever she spoke to Jasper, it seemed as if he and his chef were fighting more than getting along. Sometimes she wondered why the pair put up with one another, but the chef was incredibly talented, and the restaurant was one of the best on the island. Presumably they were both benefiting from the arrangement, whatever their personal differences.

There were only a handful of people in the restaurant, spread out across the large room. Bessie and Andrew were shown to a table in one corner and handed menus. "I'll tell you about today's specials when I bring your drinks," the waiter told them.

"I think I'm going to have the chicken, since Jasper recommended it so highly," Bessie told Andrew.

"I probably will as well, but first I want to hear exactly what it is," he replied.

After the waiter had described the dish, both Bessie and Andrew were convinced. While they waited for the food to arrive, they talked about Bessie's conversation with Grace that morning.

"I could conduct a very discreet investigation," Andrew offered after Bessie had told him the story.

"I may ask you to do that. Let me see what happens when I ring the bank tomorrow. It's entirely possible that I'll get to speak to Erica. Maybe she's avoiding Grace for some reason."

"I can't imagine why anyone would avoid Grace. She's such a lovely woman."

They were enjoying their meals when Jasper walked into the room. Bessie had her back to the door, but she guessed that he'd arrived when all the waiters in the room suddenly stood to attention and began to bustle about purposefully.

"Is that Jasper?" she asked Andrew.

He nodded. "Doesn't everyone look busy?"

Bessie laughed. "It isn't as if they were simply standing

around before he arrived. They've all been working very hard."

"That's good to hear," Jasper said as he slid into the seat next to Bessie. "I suspect your waiter is about to get a good deal more attentive."

The words were barely out of Jasper's mouth when their waiter appeared at Bessie's side.

"Can I get anyone anything?" he asked, seemingly deliberately not looking at Jasper.

"Jasper, did you want anything?" Bessie asked her friend.

He shook his head. "I had lunch before I went out. If I eat anything else, I'll end up napping in my office all afternoon." He laughed heartily and then leaned closer to Bessie. "I'll probably do that anyway," he said in a confiding tone as the waiter walked away.

"You were right about the chicken," Bessie told him.

"I'm glad you're enjoying it," he replied.

"But what did you want to ask me?" Bessie wondered.

"You know both of them. How likely do you think it is that Elizabeth Quayle and Andy Caine will get back together?" Jasper asked.

Bessie stared at him for a minute. Maybe she should have been expecting the question, but she hadn't. "I've no idea," she said after a long pause. "He's engaged to someone else, though."

Jasper nodded. "Jennifer Johnson, who is no longer being permitted to book events at the Seaview. I can't see the relationship lasting, though. Andy's too smart to stay involved with a woman who'd use such questionable business practices. He'll learn, soon enough, that she can't be trusted."

"Even if they do split up, I'm not certain that he's interested in resuming his relationship with Elizabeth. I've no idea how she feels, either," Bessie said.

"I'm not just being nosy," Jasper told her. "Elizabeth has

proposed that we develop a close professional relationship. Basically, we'd offer her services whenever anyone booked an event space here, and she'd make the Seaview the first place she'd recommend to anyone wanting to plan an event with her. Additionally, she's interested in working with our chef on events here, but also on events at other locations. I was always pleased with her work when she held events here before she went away, but I'm trying to understand what's going on in her personal life, because it may affect her business."

"I spoke to her earlier today, and I don't think you have anything to worry about," Bessie told him. "The Elizabeth that has come back from her extended holiday seems a good deal more focussed on making a success of her business than she was previously. It's possible that having a bit of competition might be good for her."

"I can't see the island supporting two party planning businesses," Jasper said.

"I believe Elizabeth is ready to fight for her business."

"And her father has enough money to keep her going for a long time. Of course, Andy Caine has a lot of money, too. If he's prepared to use his fortune to keep Jennifer in business no matter what, things could get ugly," Jasper suggested.

"Let's hope it doesn't come to that," Bessie said, thinking that she needed a long talk with Andy and without Jennifer.

The waiter cleared away their plates and brought them pudding menus. Bessie couldn't resist the jam roly-poly, and Andrew let himself be talked into a slice as well.

"I didn't have pudding earlier, so I'll have a slice, too," Jasper told the man.

The trio chatted about puddings while they ate. When Andrew asked for the bill, Jasper waved a hand. "Lunch is my treat today, since I invited myself along," he told them.

Both Bessie and Andrew tried to object, but Jasper

refused to listen. Eventually they gave up, and let Jasper lead them to the conference room where the day's meeting was being held.

"I thought you might enjoy a different location today," he told them as they walked. "As we've nothing else going on, I've put you in the penthouse meeting room."

They rode the lift to the top floor and then followed Jasper to the room at the end of the corridor.

"What incredible views," Bessie sighed as she walked into the room.

The back wall had several large windows that showcased the beach and the sea several storeys below them.

"It's stunning," Andrew agreed.

"We'll all be distracted," Doona suggested as she and John joined them.

"I hope you aren't too distracted," Andrew said. "I've a lot to tell you about our suspects and where they are now."

CHAPTER 8

*J*asper and his catering department had filled a large table with various snacks. Bessie began to regret her pudding as she looked over the small cakes, biscuits, and other sweet treats. Doona filled a plate with one of just about everything.

"I didn't get lunch," she told Bessie.

"I'm sorry that I did," Bessie sighed, taking only a few of the things that she simply couldn't resist. She poured herself a cup of tea and then took a seat facing towards the windows. "I want to be in this room every time," she told Andrew.

"It's a wonderful view," he said as he took the chair at the head of the table. He'd have to turn his head to look out at the sea, but as he was in charge of the meeting, he needed to be there.

Hugh arrived only a few minutes later. Harry and Charles turned up together about five minutes after that. Hugh filled a plate with more food than Bessie thought ought to fit. Charles got himself a cup of coffee but nothing else. Harry didn't get anything. He looked around the room and then walked around the table, choosing a seat so that he'd have his back to the windows but would be facing the door.

"You can't see the view," Bessie said.

He shrugged. "I have a similar view from my room."

"Are we ready to begin?" Andrew asked as Charles sat down next to Harry.

"Yes, please. Where are they all now?" Doona demanded.

"When we're done, I'm going to give you each copies of the recent interviews that the police had with each of the suspects. For now, let's go through them one at a time," Andrew replied. "I'd like to hear what you think happened to each of them before I tell you what really happened. It could be quite telling if someone has done something wildly different to what you all expected for him or her."

"If we're going to talk about all of them separately, does that mean that Harvey and Mary Ellen didn't end up getting married to one another?" Bessie asked.

"They did not," Andrew confirmed. "Or at least not yet. I've heard of cases where former couples reconnect after years apart and end up getting married. I suppose that's a possibility for Harvey and Mary Ellen."

"But they aren't together right now," Bessie said thoughtfully as she made herself a note.

"Let's start with Harvey," Andrew suggested. "You all read his statement and the ones from his parents. Fifteen years after the murder, where do you think he is now?"

"He'll be a lawyer," Doona guessed. "Probably working for his father's law firm. I expect he's married with two spoiled children, a boy and girl, and they'll have a dog and probably some fish."

Everyone laughed. "I don't believe anyone was asked about his or her pets," Andrew said. "Anyone else have any thoughts on where Harvey is now?"

"I imagine he's still living in Greenview," Bessie said. "Maybe in a house near his parents' house."

"If he did kill Julie, he'll have made sure to behave in ways that were exactly what was expected of him," Harry said. "He wouldn't have wanted anyone to think that he was behaving oddly."

Andrew nodded. "I know what you mean, and I agree. Does anyone else have anything to add?"

"These chocolate biscuits are delicious," Doona said. "I know that doesn't help with the case, but I thought you all should know before I go back and take all of the rest."

"And now we'll take a short break to get biscuits," Andrew told them.

A few minutes later everyone but Harry had a plate with at least one chocolate biscuit on it, and they were ready to resume.

"Harvey went to his Ivy League school and just barely graduated after five years. In spite of his less-than-stellar performance there, he was accepted to the same law school that his father had attended and managed to make it through with only one extra semester of work required. It took him six attempts to pass the bar exam, during which time he worked for his father's firm as some sort of legal assistant."

"Six times?" Doona asked. "Is that typical?"

"I don't believe so," Andrew replied.

"Is he still working for his father, then?" Bessie asked.

"He is. The firm used to handle a mix of legal issues, mostly to do with the needs of residents of a small town. They could prepare your will, help you sell your house, deal with your divorce, draw up a trust fund for your grandchild, whatever. The firm's focus now is on personal injuries."

"Personal injuries?" Hugh echoed.

"If you slip and fall outside of a shop, they'll help you sue the shop's owners for millions," Andrew told him. "If you're injured in a car accident, they'll help you sue the other driver, again for millions. They do similar things for people hurt while working at or visiting other people's houses."

Bessie frowned. "I understand those sorts of lawsuits are becoming increasingly common in the US."

"They are," Andrew agreed. "Law firms are allowed to advertise their services, and apparently they brag in those ads about the millions they've been able to get for people. I understand insurance is getting more and more expensive all the time as people sue over every little thing."

"And that's what Harvey and his father are doing now?" Bessie checked.

"It is. Mary Ellen's father left the firm and set up on his own over ten years ago, before Harvey came back to Greenview. He's still doing the same sort of work that he'd been doing for years, mostly preparing wills and helping people buy and sell homes," Andrew told her.

"And is Harvey married?" Doona wondered.

"He's been married and divorced twice. No children," Andrew replied. "His last divorce took place three months ago, and he's now staying in what's called an in-law suite in his parents' house."

"What's an in-law suite?" Hugh asked.

"A separate bedroom, bathroom, and small kitchen within a larger home," Andrew explained. "It has its own entrance, so Harvey can come and go as he pleases, but it means his mother can wash his clothes for him and make him dinner every night."

Bessie made a noise. "His mother washes his clothes?"

"She's never gone back to work. According to Harvey, she doesn't have anything else to do besides look after him and his father."

"That poor woman," Bessie muttered.

"So he's living with his parents, working as a lawyer,"

Doona said. "It sounds as if he's doing exactly what he'd planned, albeit without the marriage to Mary Ellen."

"She wasn't one of his wives?" Charles checked.

"She was not. His first wife was a woman he'd met in law school. She'd dropped out after a year, but they got married while he was still studying. They were divorced before he graduated. His second wife was hired as a law clerk at the firm about three years ago. She wasn't from Greenview. She'd moved there with her husband, whom she divorced six months later. She and Harvey were married as soon as her divorce was final."

"And they got divorced just over two years later," Bessie said, hoping she'd done the maths correctly.

"That's about right," Andrew agreed. "He said they'd simply grown apart."

"The police need to speak to her," Harry said. "They need to find out what really happened. I'm mostly interested in whether or not Harvey cheats."

Andrew nodded and made a note. "I'm going to ask them to try to find the first wife, too. And now I think we should move on. Let's talk about Mary Ellen next. Her future was supposed to be tied up with Harvey's. Anyone want to guess what happened to Mary Ellen?"

"She went to law school and now fights for women's rights in Washington, DC," Doona said. "At least, that's what I hope she's doing."

"I can see her being badly affected by the murder," Harry said. "When I read her interview, I didn't get the impression that she was eager to become a lawyer and follow in her father's footsteps. She was doing what she'd been told she was meant to do. I can see the murder changing her thinking on a lot of things. It wouldn't surprise me to hear that she moved to Wisconsin to run a dairy farm or something."

Andrew grinned at him. "Anyone else?"

"She seemed quite intelligent," Bessie remarked. "Maybe she decided to study something else that interested her, archeology or economics or something else completely different."

"She went off to school as expected," Andrew told them. "She even did well in her first semester, earning good grades and making new friends. After the Christmas holidays, she went back and had, as she described it, something of a breakdown. She failed all of her classes in the second semester and then dropped out of school. According to her statement, she made her way across the country, staying in different places, wherever the wind took her, or so she claimed. Eventually she ended up in Colorado where she was able to get a job at a ski resort."

"Her parents had a holiday home at a ski resort, didn't they?" Hugh remembered.

"Yes, in the Poconos in Pennsylvania," Andrew agreed. "Her mother said that Mary Ellen had been skiing since she'd been walking."

"What sort of job?" Bessie asked.

"She started out working in the lodge, signing people up for lessons and that sort of thing. After a while, she started teaching lessons, and that's what she's doing now. She's one of their most popular instructors, but she isn't always the most reliable employee. She keeps her job because she's so good at it, but she admitted to drinking too much and calling off sick fairly regularly."

"Oh, dear," Bessie said.

"She goes by M.E. now, rather than Mary Ellen, and she's currently living with another of the instructors," Andrew added.

"Living with?" Doona repeated. "Are they romantically involved, as well?"

"They are," Andrew confirmed. "He's fifty-six and legally married to a woman living somewhere in California."

"Mary Ellen has never been married?" Bessie asked.

"She has not. You can read it for yourself, but when asked about marriage, she said something about being 'a free spirit who wasn't interested in being tied down to conventional society's determination of appropriate relationship goals,'" Andrew told her.

"So she's living with a married man and drinking too much," Harry said. "Is it possible that guilt is eating away at her?"

"See how you feel once you've read her interview," Andrew suggested. "She seems quite happy with the way her life is going, actually."

"Did the police speak to her parents again?" Doona wondered. "I'd love to know what her mother thinks of all of this."

"Mary Ellen's father spoke to the police, but requested that they not try to speak to her mother. She's been fighting cancer for the last eighteen months, and he didn't want to add to the stress that she's been under."

"What did he have to say about Mary Ellen?" Bessie asked.

"That they were still very proud of their daughter, even if she hadn't done what they might have wanted her to do with her life. And that there was no way that she'd had anything to do with Julie's murder, of course," Andrew said.

"Well, I'm disappointed in her," Bessie said. "As I said, she seemed quite smart. I thought that she'd do well once she got away from Harvey and her mother."

"By her definition, she is doing quite well," Andrew replied.

Bessie nodded. "If she's happy, then maybe she's smarter than I realised."

"Let's talk about Jack next," Andrew said. "He was going

to study biology and then become a doctor, the same as his father. Anyone want to speculate on what really happened?"

"He didn't seem interesting enough to do anything wildly different," Doona said. "That sounds mean, but it isn't meant to be. He simply didn't seem to have much imagination, if you know what I mean."

"His mother passed away a year later, though," Bessie remembered. "That may have resulted in him changing his plans in some way."

"I don't think his mother's death was what made him change his plans," Andrew said. "In his recent interview, he credited what he saw after Julie's death with why he ended up doing something rather different with his life."

"So where is he now?" Doona demanded as Andrew stopped for a sip of tea.

"He studied biology in college and then went to medical school, all according to his original plan. Then he quit medical school and trained as a crime scene investigator."

"Interesting," Harry said.

"He's been working in New York City for the past six years," Andrew told them. "He's built up a reputation as an expert in stab wounds."

"Very interesting," Harry remarked.

"I suppose I can see how what happened at the cabin might have led to his becoming interested in the subject," Bessie said thoughtfully.

"What about his personal life?" Charles asked.

"He got married just before he dropped out of medical school. The marriage ended less than a year later. In his interview, he explains that she wanted to be married to a doctor more than she wanted to be married to him," Andrew replied.

"And he hasn't remarried?" Bessie wondered.

"He has not, although he does have a partner, and they

live together. They have a small flat in New York City. His partner also works for the police there. She's a homicide detective. They met through work," Andrew told them.

"Does his being with the police now move him up or down the list of suspects?" Bessie asked.

Andrew shrugged. "That's a very good question. The detective that interviewed him recently didn't seem to care for him. In his notes, he suggested that Jack was so good at his job because he had firsthand experience with murder."

"I wonder why the detective disliked him," Bessie said.

"You may not wonder after you read the interview," Andrew told her. "When I read it, I felt very much as if there was simply a large personality clash between the two men. You'll have to see what you think."

Bessie nodded. "He doesn't have any children?"

"Not yet, anyway," Andrew replied.

"When I read the first interviews, I thought it seemed as if Jack was pretty head over heels in love with Katie," Bessie said. "I'm a bit sad that they didn't end up together. I can't remember now what Katie was planning after high school."

"She'd been awarded a generous scholarship to a small private liberal arts college in Maryland. She'd wanted to study international politics and French and work for the United Nations one day," Andrew reminded her.

Bessie nodded. "I remember reading it, but I don't know that we discussed it before. Whatever, I'm going to guess that she did exactly what she said she was going to do."

"Anyone else want to guess where Katie is now?" Andrew asked.

"She seemed so intimidated by everyone around her who had any money, I can see her being overwhelmed at a school where most of the students were from wealthy backgrounds," Harry said. "I can imagine her dropping out and moving back to Greenview."

"She did drop out," Andrew said. "But not because she was intimidated by her wealthy classmates. She dropped out because she fell pregnant."

"Oh, dear," Bessie exclaimed. "The poor girl."

Andrew chuckled. "Except she isn't at all poor. She quit school and got married immediately to the father of the child. He was from a very wealthy family and Katie, now calling herself Katherine, appears to have been welcomed with open arms. They've had seven children so far and, in her police interview, Katherine said they were considering adding one more to the family. Of course, they have several nannies and other staff to help with all of the work involved in bringing up a large family."

"I'm going to guess that she hasn't gone back to school, then," Bessie said.

"Actually, she earned her first degree by going to school part-time over six years. It took her four more years to earn her Masters degree, and she's now working on a doctorate," Andrew told her. "Her degrees are both in history, specifically American history, with an emphasis on the role of women in the history of the country. That's the focus of her doctoral research as well."

"Good for her. I can't imagine doing all of that while having seven children, but then, I can't imagine having seven children," Doona said.

"I don't know what that tells us about her," Harry said. "I mean, in terms of the likelihood of her having murdered Julie."

"You may feel otherwise after you read the complete interview," Andrew said.

"That just leaves Mike," John said. "On the surface, he seemed the mostly likely suspect. He'd had a fight with the victim, and he was the only person sleeping alone."

"He was going somewhere on a football scholarship, wasn't he?" Bessie remembered.

"He was. Anyone want to guess what happened to him?" Andrew asked.

"He was so distraught about the murder that he decided to take a year out to recover, except he still hasn't managed to recover and is living in his parents' basement drinking or doing drugs all day," Charles guessed.

"I thought he sounded as if he was a nice young man," Bessie countered. "I can imagine him going to college and working hard at football."

"Bessie's closer," Andrew told them. "He did go to college as planned, and he played football for two years. Then he suffered an injury that meant he couldn't play any longer. The detective I spoke to told me that a lot of kids quit school at that point, because they lose their scholarships and don't have any plans beyond that, but Mike transferred to a much less expensive school and finished his degree."

"Good for him," Bessie said.

"He started working as an assistant football coach for a local high school team while he was still in college, and he's still working with high school teams in the city where he's now living. According to the detective in Pennsylvania, he's a very successful businessman," Andrew added.

"Family?" Charles wondered.

"He's married, and he and his wife have three children. They have two boys and a girl, with the girl being the middle child," Andrew told him.

"And that's everyone, since we all know what happened to Julie," Harry said in a low voice.

CHAPTER 9

"I know you told us that there wasn't anything in the updated information that would definitely help with the case, but I was really hoping you were wrong," Bessie sighed.

"It's interesting that Mary Ellen went in such a different direction," Charles said. "I thought, before we started today, that anyone doing anything vastly different from his or her original plans would warrant a closer look."

"In her interview, she said that Julie's death had taught her that life is short, too short to waste time doing things that you don't love," Andrew replied. "She said she was surprised that none of her other former friends had done anything interesting with their lives, having lived through the same tragedy with her."

"Jack is doing something rather different than his original plan," Doona said.

Andrew nodded. "But it wasn't until some years after Julie's death, while he was in medical school, that he decided to pursue a different path."

"And now he's an expert in stab wounds," John said.

"Which one of the suspects was enough of an expert to stab Julie in just the right place, though? If the reports are correct, she was killed instantly, and the killer had time to get out of the way to avoid getting covered in blood. That seems as if it would need some specialist knowledge."

"I asked the detective in Pennsylvania about that. Five of the six of them had taken an anatomy class together at the local community college. It was one of only a handful of classes that were available to high school students. Apparently that meant that even the ones who weren't especially interested in anatomy took the class because they wanted a few college credits on their high school transcripts," Andrew told them.

"Which one of the six didn't take the class?" Bessie asked.

"Julie," Andrew replied.

Bessie frowned. "So any one of them could have known enough about anatomy to stab Julie in just the right place."

"The killer may have simply been lucky, rather than smart, too," Hugh added.

Andrew nodded. "And we can't discount the idea that he or she was, well, naked. It's possible that the killer did get covered in blood and then simply showered it away."

"Aren't there ways to look for blood residue in the showers?" Doona asked.

"There are. I don't know what was available to the police force in Greenview in those days, but no such tests were run," Andrew told her.

"What are the chances of someone hitting just the right spot in that way?" Bessie asked. "I know Hugh said the killer may have been lucky, but surely it's not that easy to stab someone and kill them with the first attempt."

"Actually, if Julie was asleep, and we've every reason to believe that she was, it may not have been that difficult. It was a large knife. All the killer needed to do was hit Julie's heart. The detective I spoke to said that he or she was about an inch lower than would have been ideal, actually, but that an inch in any direction would still have been fatal," Andrew told her.

"The knife came out of the kitchen?" Hugh asked. "I'm sure that was covered somewhere in the files, but I've forgotten now."

"Yes, it came out of the kitchen," John replied, flipping through his notes. "It was part of a set in a knife block in the kitchen. There were meant to be ten knives in the block, but two were missing when the police searched the house after the murder. According to Mary Ellen's parents, one of the knives had been lost or damaged and thrown away years earlier. The other missing knife was the murder weapon."

"And everyone had access to the kitchen," Doona sighed. "They were even taking turns cooking."

"Or not, in Harvey's case," Bessie said. "I can't believe he didn't do anything to help the entire weekend, but that was how it seemed when I read the files."

"I don't remember reading about him doing anything other than drinking and watching movies," Doona said.

"What about fingerprints?" Hugh asked. "I mean, I assume they weren't able to get any useful ones from the murder weapon, or we wouldn't be talking about the case."

Andrew nodded. "There were partial prints on the handle of the knife, but none were complete enough to be used as evidence. Everyone in the house, aside from Harvey, anyway, could have argued that he or she had touched the knife while helping in the kitchen, though."

"So fingerprints are a dead end," Hugh sighed.

"So, what does everyone think?" Andrew asked. "I haven't gone back to the police in Pennsylvania with any questions yet. I know you haven't read the recent statements, but do you have any questions for them to ask the suspects, or anything you want clarified by the police themselves?"

"I think they should look most closely at Mary Ellen," Harry said. "Julie's death seems to have made her change her plans the most radically."

"They should look at Jack for the same reason," Charles said. "He ended up doing something different because of Julie's murder, too."

"I still don't care for Harvey," Bessie said.

"And Bessie is usually right with her suspicions," Harry said. "Forget what I said. Tell the police to focus on Harvey."

Bessie shook her head. "I agree that Mary Ellen and Jack should also be considered," she said. "I just wish I had some idea of what the police should ask them all."

"It would helpful if they could try to pin down the timeline more closely," John suggested. "I know the suspects were all drinking and probably not paying much attention to the time, but it might be useful to ask them all to try to write out a timeline of events for the entire weekend. I'd really like to compare their replies."

Andrew nodded. "That's a excellent idea. Of course, how much anyone will remember after all these years is another matter, but it may be worth a try."

"Which of them are still in contact with any of the others?" Doona asked. "Do they ever see one another? None of them are living in the same place, are they?"

"No, although Harvey is in Greenview, and all of the parents are still there. I assume everyone comes back to visit now and again," Andrew said, making a note.

"Presumably they have reunions," Charles said. "I understand American schools always do. Which of the five attend them?"

Andrew added that question to his notes. "In the recent interviews, I believe they were all asked when they last saw one another, but I don't think they were pushed for any details. It's an interesting question."

"A traumatic event such as a murder can either bring groups of friends together or drive them apart," Harry said.

"But were they even friends?" Bessie asked. "I'm not clear on which of them were friends, actually. We talked about how Mike and Harvey were on the football team together. I assume there were a dozen or more men on the team, though. Why was Mike invited for the weekend over any of the others? Maybe that's something for them to ask Mary Ellen. Exactly how was the guest list created?"

"It did come up in the original statements," John said. "But Mary Ellen's answers were vague. She said something about inviting the people she wanted to be with."

Bessie nodded. "It's a small town, and I assume everyone knows everyone, or nearly. No doubt the local police knew the six students and their entire life histories, but I'm curious about the relationships between the young people. Mary Ellen and Harvey had been together for years. Did they never fight? Was it possible that they'd broken up from time to time? The other two couples had been together for much shorter periods of time. Is it possible that any of the others had a romantic history prior to graduation weekend?"

"Those are good questions and not ones that were ever asked, as far as I can remember. As you say, the detective doing the investigating may have known the men and women well enough to not have had to ask. I'll see what I can find out, though," Andrew said, adding her question to his list.

"We always talk in terms of means, motive, and opportunity," Hugh said. "In this case, they all seemed to have had the means and the opportunity. I wonder about motive, though. Why did any of them want to kill Julie Carter?"

"She and Mike were fighting about something," Harry

said. "It would be really helpful to know what that something was."

"In his statement, Mike kept insisting that it was just a stupid disagreement over nothing that was fuelled by too much alcohol," Andrew told him. "That may be true, of course, but people have been killed over less."

"It was bad enough to make Julie want to sleep on the couch in the living room," Bessie said. "Why do I think that, if she were still alive, she'd be able to tell us exactly what the fight was about?"

"You think Mike is lying?" Andrew asked.

"I think they're all hiding what they know about that fight," Bessie said. "Maybe we'll learn more if they all put those timelines together. Maybe someone will end up having to admit to having overheard the argument."

"He or she will simply claim to have been too drunk to follow what was being said," Doona predicted. "I'm sort of surprised at how they all seemed to want to cover for one another in their initial interviews. Has that changed much in the second set of interviews?" she asked Andrew.

"Not at all. Everyone says much the same thing about being too drunk to have been able to keep track of everyone else, but that there's no way any of them killed Julie," Andrew replied. "Even Mary Ellen, who was the one who initially said it couldn't have been anyone from outside."

"I thought Mary Ellen always claimed that she didn't actually drink that much that weekend," Bessie said.

"In her initial interview, she did say that, but in her later one, she does admit to having drunk quite a lot over the weekend," Andrew told her.

Bessie sighed. "Someone has to know something or have seen something. Maybe something he or she doesn't even realise is significant. The timelines may be a big help."

"And time may be on our side," Harry added. "After

fifteen years, the men and women involved may be less likely to try to protect one another than they were years ago."

Andrew nodded. "You all have the new interviews to read. We'll meet again on Tuesday to discuss what's in them. I hope to have some answers to some of your questions by that time, as well."

"I wonder if there isn't someone outside of the case who can help," Bessie said thoughtfully.

"What do you mean?" Andrew asked.

"I mean someone else from that graduating class, someone who knew all six of the people who were in that cabin that weekend. Maybe someone the police know will be truthful about those people and the relationships between them. We've heard from all of the parents, of course, and a few coaches and other adults who knew the young men and women. I wonder if one of their contemporaries could give us a different angle on the case," Bessie explained.

"I'll ask," Andrew told her.

"So, two o'clock on Tuesday?" Harry checked.

"Yes, that's right," Andrew agreed.

"See you then," Charles said, grabbing his paperwork and rushing out of the room.

"What's the most interesting thing to see on the island?" Harry asked Bessie.

She flushed. "I've no idea what you'd consider interesting," she replied.

He shrugged. "Something historical, maybe. A museum, perhaps."

"The House of Manannan in Peel is a wonderful museum," she told him. "You'll get a brief history of the island through interactive displays and stories."

"Would you care to accompany me there tomorrow?" he asked.

Bessie hesitated and then nodded. "I always enjoy a trip around the House of Manannan," she told him.

"What time do they open?" he asked.

"Ten o'clock," she replied.

"I'll collect you from your cottage at half nine, then," he said. "I hope we'll be able to find somewhere for lunch after our tour?"

"There's a small café in the museum, or there are several pubs in the area around it," she told him.

"Pub lunch it is," he said with a small smile. "You're all welcome to join us, of course," he told the others.

"I may," Andrew said. "I don't have plans for tomorrow."

"I'll be working," Hugh said.

"Me too," John added.

"And I already have plans for the day," Doona told him. "Thank you anyway."

Harry nodded and then stood up, picking up his envelope as he did so. "I'd better get busy with these reports then, so I can enjoy the museum tomorrow with a clear conscience." He left the room before anyone could reply.

"Are you certain you want to go around the House of Manannan with him?" Doona asked as the door shut behind the man.

Bessie nodded. "You know I always encourage everyone to learn more about the island and its rich history. I'm delighted that he's interested in doing so."

Doona didn't look convinced, but she didn't argue. They all gathered their things and headed out of the room as a group.

"I hope we can use that room again next time," Bessie said in the lift on the way down to the foyer.

"I'll ask Jasper," Andrew told her. "I'm sure he'll accommodate us if he can."

They got the chance to find out only a moment later as

they found Jasper in the foyer, rearranging furniture. The others all left as Bessie and Andrew crossed over to the hotel's manager.

"Try a little to the left," he was telling the two burly men who were carrying a large couch.

Jasper watched as they moved the piece of furniture. "More, more, more, stop," he said. Then he sighed. "No, back to the right, more, more, just there."

"I hate to interrupt," Bessie said, touching Jasper's arm. "But we wanted to thank you for letting us use that amazing room today."

"Oh, please interrupt," Jasper told her with a small laugh. "I had a horrible disagreement with Stuart. Then Chef and I nearly came to blows over the new dinner menu, and we've had three guests cancel their summer bookings in the last half hour. I'm so frustrated that I'm moving furniture that's absolutely fine exactly where it is."

"I am sorry," Bessie told him, giving him a hug. "Can I help in any way?" she asked as she released him.

"It's all fine, really," he replied. "I'm glad you enjoyed the penthouse conference room. You're welcome to use it every time you meet here, at least until we get busy again, assuming we ever get busy again."

"We'd like the space for all of our meetings for the foreseeable future," Andrew told him.

"I'll make a note in your file," Jasper promised. "At the moment, I'm certain I'll remember, but we may get busy one day and I may forget. That's why I make so many notes."

Andrew nodded. "We'll be back on Tuesday afternoon."

"Splendid. I look forward to seeing you again," Jasper said.

As Bessie and Andrew began to walk away, Jasper turned back around. "Just another inch to the left," he told the two men.

Bessie could hear one of them sigh with frustration as she and Andrew walked through the doors.

"Home?" Andrew asked as he helped Bessie into his hire car.

"I suppose so," she said.

"You didn't sound certain just then," he told her once he was behind the wheel.

"I've a great deal to do at home, including reading through all of the recent interviews you've just given us, but I'm feeling a bit, I don't know, restless, maybe," she admitted.

"Where should we go, then?"

A loud ringing noise startled them both. "It's my mobile phone," Bessie sighed. "Now I just have to find it."

The ringing continued as she dug around in her handbag, unable to locate the device. She'd only just pulled it out of the bag when it suddenly stopped.

"Oh, bother," she muttered, staring at the screen.

"Do you recognise the number that rang?" Andrew asked.

Bessie pushed a few buttons until she was able to see who had rung. "It was Mark Blake from Manx National Heritage," she told him. "It's probably something to do with Christmas at the Castle, although he doesn't normally ring me on a Sunday about that."

"Ring him back," Andrew suggested.

Bessie nodded and then tapped in his number.

"Ah, Bessie, thank you for ringing back," Mark said a moment later. "We're having a small issue with one of our suppliers, and I was hoping you'd have time to come down to Castletown to discuss strategies with me."

"Today?"

"Not necessarily today, but I'm available today if you are. Otherwise, tomorrow would do, but I'm going to need to have some answers before Tuesday if we're going to stay on schedule."

"This all sounds serious. Are you trying to get the entire committee together?"

"At the moment, you are the entire committee," he told her. "There were four of you, but one person quit, another is ill, and the third is off-island right now. That just leaves you and me to make decisions."

"Give me a moment," Bessie said. She looked at Andrew. "How about a visit to Castletown?" she asked. "Mark needs to speak with me about some issues that have arisen."

"We can do that," he agreed. "I'll poke around the castle while you meet, if that's allowed."

"Mark, I can be at the castle in forty minutes or so. We're in Ramsey now. Assuming we need to meet at the castle, that is."

"We do, as you'll need to see what's been done thus far before we can make any decisions about what to do next. I'll see you at the castle shortly, then. And thank you."

He ended the call before Bessie could ask if he minded if Andrew looked around the castle while they talked, but that wasn't worth ringing him back to ask. Instead, she buckled her seatbelt, and Andrew headed for Castletown.

"Of course Andrew can look around," Mark said when they found him at the castle doors. "Or he can come with us and offer his opinion on everything. Whichever he'd prefer."

"I'll just have a quick walk through the building first," Andrew replied. "I don't get here very often, after all. I'm sure Bessie's opinion will be exactly what you need, anyway."

Two hours later, Andrew found Mark and Bessie in the throne room.

"This is where I would spend all of my time if I owned the castle," Andrew told them as he looked around the large space.

"Did you enjoy your tour?" Bessie asked.

"It was lovely. Have you given many opinions?" he replied.

Bessie laughed. "Quite a few and, fortunately, they nearly all agreed with Mark's opinions."

"Thank you both for taking the time to come down here tonight. Let me buy you dinner to thank you," Mark suggested.

"We don't eat in Castletown very often," Andrew said. "Is there somewhere nearby that does good food?"

"There are a great many places," Mark told him.

Bessie let the men choose a location for dinner. She knew she'd be eating many meals in Castletown each week later in the month as planning for Christmas at the Castle became more intense. For tonight, she'd be happy eating anywhere.

After a delicious meal, Andrew drove them back to Laxey at a leisurely pace.

"And now I'm off to send a long email to my colleague in Pennsylvania," he told Bessie after he'd checked that everything was as it should be at her cottage. "I'll ask him to request a timeline for the weekend from each of the witnesses, ask about their relationships in the past and in the present, and see if he knows of anyone who went to school with the six men and women and can tell us more about them."

"I suspect he isn't going to be happy to get your email," Bessie replied.

Andrew chuckled. "He asked for our help. He shouldn't complain when we ask for more information."

"I wonder what the suspects are going to think when they get asked to try to create timelines."

"I'm hoping they'll think that now would be a good time to be completely honest about what happened in that cabin all those years ago," Andrew told her. "But I doubt this is going to be that easy."

CHAPTER 10

Heavy rain made Bessie cut her walk short the next morning. "At least we're going to the House of Manannan and not Peel Castle," she told her reflection as she dried her hair and face. It was just a few minutes after nine when she rang the bank in Liverpool.

"Ah, yes, good morning," she said when someone answered. "I need to speak to someone in the lending department. I'm thinking about buying a house in Liverpool."

"Certainly, let me connect you to Donald Plant. He's one of our lending advisors," the voice said.

"Oh, but, I mean, I was speaking to someone the other day, someone here, and they recommended that I ask for Erica Tucker. I gather she was able to help my friend a great deal."

"I'm awfully sorry, but Ms. Tucker isn't in today. I can assure you, though, that Mr. Plant will be able to do anything that Ms. Tucker could."

"Will Ms. Tucker be there tomorrow? I'm sorry to be difficult, but she came so highly recommended, you see."

"I'm not certain when Ms. Tucker will next be in the office. I don't have access to her schedule."

"Can I leave a message with you, asking her to ring me?" Bessie asked.

"I suggest that you speak with Mr. Plant," the woman replied, sounding slightly annoyed. "He can answer your initial questions and start taking the information we'll need. The entire application can be transferred to Ms. Tucker when she's next available."

"I'm not certain what to do. I think I'll ring back tomorrow and see if Ms. Tucker is available." She put the phone down before the woman on the other end could argue.

The last thing Bessie wanted to do was ring Grace and tell her that she'd failed to find her friend, but Grace needed to know.

"Did she sound worried about Erica?" Grace asked after Bessie had recounted the conversation.

"Not at all. She simply said she wasn't available. Maybe Erica has the day off."

"Maybe. I'd feel a good deal better if she'd told you to ring back tomorrow, though."

"Yes, well, I will ring back tomorrow. In the meantime, if you think of anything else I can do, please let me know."

"I was wondering if I should try ringing her ex-boyfriend," Grace said slowly. "He's here on the island. I've never met him, but she told me a lot about him."

"Tell me about him," Bessie suggested.

"I should have told you about him yesterday. I didn't really think of him until yesterday afternoon, though. They went out for about a year when Erica was in her late teens, and they've stayed friends ever since. Erica told me once that he was the only person in the world that she trusted completely."

"What else do you know about him?" Bessie asked when Grace fell silent.

"He's a few years older than Erica. They met in a Shop-Fast car park. She very nearly hit his car when she was reversing out of a space. He was really nice about it, and after she was done apologising, he asked her out. As I said, they went out for about a year before she ended things."

"She ended things?"

"Yes, because she didn't think the relationship was going anywhere. He felt they were too young to get married, and she didn't see the point in staying together if they weren't planning to get married at some point."

"Did he not want to marry her at all, or just not yet?" Bessie asked.

"He said it was just not yet, but he wouldn't get engaged, either. She didn't want to give him an ultimatum just to get a ring on her finger, so she ended things."

"But they've remained friends?"

"That's what Erica told me, anyway. I sort of felt as if she still thought they might get back together one day, even though she's seen lots of other guys since she ended things with him."

"What's his name?"

"Oh, sorry — Ian Branson. He lives in Douglas, or he did the last time Erica mentioned him."

"What does he do?"

"He's an electrician."

"Maybe you should ring him."

"I don't have any idea what to say," Grace sighed. "I don't want to tell him that I think Erica is missing, not when she could be off with a new boyfriend somewhere. The last thing I want is Ian, her ex-boyfriend, disturbing her romantic weekend away, if that's where she is."

"So you need to think of another reason to ring Ian," Bessie said thoughtfully. "When is Erica's birthday?"

"June, I think. I have it written down somewhere. I can go and check."

"It doesn't matter. What if you rang Ian and said that you were trying to plan a surprise birthday party for her? You could try to sound him out to see if he's spoken to her lately."

"It's a great idea, but I'm not certain I could do it," Grace replied. "I'm a terrible liar."

"Even over the telephone?"

"Even over the telephone," Grace sighed "I start to giggle or cry, one or the other, and then I can't talk. I don't suppose you could ring Ian?"

"I could, but I can't imagine what excuse I could use. I'd hardly be planning a party for Erica, since I've never even met her."

"What about her mother?"

"What about her mother? I thought you said she had memory problems?" Bessie said questioningly.

"She does, but what if you were planning a party for Erica's mother? Maybe you could be an old friend of hers, wanting to have a party for her soon, before she gets any worse. You could be inviting all of Erica's friends to the party."

"I think this is getting far too complicated," Bessie told her. "Why don't you have Hugh ring someone in Liverpool and ask that someone to make discreet inquiries?"

"Maybe, if I haven't heard anything by Wednesday," Grace replied. "I don't suppose you need anything rewiring at your cottage?"

"Rewiring?"

"Or maybe a new light fitting installed or something? Something that you'd need an electrician to do," Grace explained.

"I don't need an electrician, and even if I did, I can't imagine how I'd turn the conversation to Erica while the man was dealing with my wires."

Grace sighed. "I'm sorry. I'm just a horrible pest."

"You aren't. You're concerned about your friend. I understand and appreciate that, but I simply don't know what I can do to help. Have a think if there's anyone else you know who is in regular contact with Erica. Does she keep in touch with any of her other former teaching colleagues? Maybe one of them has heard from her in the last few days."

"That's a great idea. I'll ring everyone I know who used to work with her. I'm certain she'll have stayed in touch with some of the other teachers."

Bessie hoped that Grace's optimism wasn't misplaced. She put the phone down and then paced around her kitchen for several minutes. Andrew arrived before she could start looking up electricians in the telephone directory.

"Ready for the House of Manannan?" he asked her.

"I always enjoy the House of Manannan," she replied.

"Are you going to be terribly upset if I don't join you?" was his next question.

"Not upset, of course, but slightly disappointed."

He nodded. "My daughter rang late last night. There's another small family crisis involving one of the grandsons, and they need my years of experience and words of wisdom, or some such thing. I have to ring each of my children and see if I can find out exactly what's happening before I can offer any words, wise or otherwise."

"I'm sorry," Bessie said.

He shrugged. "I love my children and their partners and their children and those partners and…" he trailed off and then laughed. "We're one big dysfunctional mess sometimes, but we all love one another. Secretly, I feel flattered when they ask for my opinion or my advice, even though they rarely seem to listen to what I say."

Another knock on the door stopped Bessie from replying.

"Good morning," Harry said brightly.

"Good morning," Bessie replied.

"Yes, good morning," Andrew said. "And now I must go. I hope you both enjoy the museum."

Harry looked surprised as he watched Andrew walk back to his cottage.

"Is something wrong?" he asked Bessie.

"A small family crisis, or so I'm told," Bessie replied.

"He does have a large family. I suppose that must mean the occasional crisis."

"You don't have a large family?" Bessie asked.

Harry frowned. "No," he said curtly.

"My family is all in America now," Bessie told him. "When my parents and I came back after our years there, all that were left here were a handful of cousins and a few more distant relatives. They've all gone, of course, and I believe all of their offspring have either passed away or moved off the island. My sister's family is all in the US. She had ten children, so I suppose I have a large family. They are just rather far away."

"Ten children?" Harry echoed. "I can't imagine."

"Neither can I. But shall we be on our way?"

"Yes, let's go," he replied.

Bessie grabbed her handbag and locked her door behind them. Harry's hire car was a small and sporty model, one that Bessie struggled slightly to climb inside. Harry made a face as he slid behind the wheel.

"I hired this car because I've always wanted to drive one. I thought it would be exciting and fun to drive, and I suppose it is, but it's also hard to get into and out of when you're a bit older. I won't make the mistake of getting it again."

"Surely you can take it back and trade it for something else."

"But that would be admitting that I'm old and out of shape," Harry countered. "I can't do that."

"I truly don't understand men."

"Neither do I."

Bessie laughed. "Do you know where you're going?"

"No, and I won't ask for directions, either."

She opened her mouth to argue, but he held up a hand. "I'm teasing. I spent some time studying the map last night. I think I can find the House of Manannan, but do tell me if I take a wrong turn, please."

"Do you want me to point out other interesting things as we pass them?"

"Yes, please. I noticed on the map that we'll be going right past Tynwald Hill. Can you see much of it from the road?"

"You can see the entire thing from the road," Bessie replied.

They chatted about the island's sites as Harry drove steadily across the island. Bessie pointed out the TT Grandstand and Tynwald Hill before they finally reached Peel.

"I wasn't expecting the roads to be this narrow, twisty, or steep," Harry said as he drove towards the museum.

"The car park is behind the building," Bessie told him as the Viking ship at the entrance came into view.

"I read about how the ship seems to be sailing through the window at the front of the building," he said, slowing down to get a better look.

The car behind them honked loudly.

"You'll be able to see it much better on our way in, anyway," Bessie told him as he was forced to speed up on his way to the car park.

The first few rooms of the museum were recreations of moments from Manx history. Bessie felt as if she'd never get tired of hearing the stories that were told in each of the rooms. When they got to the last of those rooms, there was clearly something wrong, though.

"I'm sorry, but there won't be a story in here today, or at least not in the next hour or so," a man in a Manx National Heritage shirt told her. "There's something wrong with the power. We've an electrician on the way. You're more than welcome to come back around after you've seen the rest of the museum."

"We'll do that," Bessie said.

She and Harry walked through the rest of the building, learning about Viking ships and herring fishing and other things before they headed back down to the room they'd missed. As they entered, a man was standing on a ladder in the centre of the room, working on something in the ceiling.

"I don't think they've finished repairing everything yet," Harry said with a chuckle.

"No, clearly not."

"Hello." The man on the ladder ducked his head out of the ceiling and grinned at them. "I'm nearly done. Give me five minutes, and then you can help me test the system, if you want."

Bessie looked at Harry. "Do you want to wait?"

"We've seen everything else. I don't imagine I'll come back again in a hurry, so yes, let's wait," he replied.

There were benches, so Bessie and Harry sat down together on one of them. Bessie could hear the man on the ladder muttering to himself as he worked. She couldn't understand most of what he was saying, but once a curse word came out loudly and clearly.

"Sorry," he shouted, bending down to give Bessie a sheepish grin. "I don't normally have an audience."

A few minutes later, he climbed part of the way down the ladder and slid a panel in the ceiling back into place. "Let's see if I actually did any good," he said to Bessie and Harry. After shutting the doors, he flipped a switch on the wall. The room went dark and a story about the island in Viking times unfolded around them. When it finished, the lights came back on and the doors swung open.

"Very good," Bessie told the man.

"I wish I'd had something to do with the design and everything, but I just reconnected the power," he replied.

Bessie got to her feet. "Well, you seem to have done that part well, anyway. Do you have a card with you, in case I ever need an electrician for anything?"

The man grinned. "Sure. I don't do a lot of household work, but if I'm not fully booked..." He trailed off as he dug around in his pockets, finally pulling out a business card.

When he handed it to Bessie, she was almost afraid to look. *There is no way I'm going to be that lucky,* she thought.

"Ian Branson," she read off the card. "Someone else gave me your name earlier today."

"Really? So you do need an electrician? Because I am really busy, but I could..."

Bessie held up a hand. "I don't need one at the moment, but thank you anyway. I was talking to my friend Grace about how I don't know any electricians any longer, and she mentioned your name. Apparently, she knows you because she's friends with Erica Tucker."

Ian shrugged. "I don't think I know anyone named Grace, but I could be wrong. As for Erica, I haven't spoken to her in months. I suppose I should be grateful that she's saying nice things about me, shouldn't I?"

"Grace said that Erica had told her that you are an excellent electrician," Bessie said, stretching the truth slightly.

"Ah, well, Erica and I, we, I don't even know what to say to that, actually."

Bessie smiled at him. "I'm just happy to have your card in

case I ever need you. And if you are too busy to do the work yourself, at least you'll be able to recommend someone else."

He nodded. "I'm usually not terribly busy this time of year, actually, but the guy who normally does all of the work for Manx National Heritage managed to fall off a ladder doing some work in his own home. He recommended me to fill in for him, and they've been keeping me running all over the island. I'll probably have more time for other jobs once he's back on his feet."

"Thank you," Bessie said, tucking the card into her handbag.

Harry had been watching her closely during the exchange. Now he offered his arm. "I believe we were going to get lunch," he said.

After a brief discussion, they agreed to go to the pub just across the street from the museum. They found a table in the back corner, and then Harry placed their order at the bar. When he came back with their drinks, he sat down opposite Bessie, his back to the wall, facing into the room.

"Do you want to tell me what the conversation with the electrician was all about?" he asked conversationally.

Bessie flushed. "Not really," she replied honestly.

He chuckled. "I'm going to guess that you're looking for this Erica Tucker you mentioned. I'm going to assume that it isn't anything serious, otherwise you'd have discussed it with your friends who are with the police."

"I am looking for Erica, yes. She hasn't been responding to text messages or phone calls from a friend of mine. My friend reckons that Erica is probably just busy, and she doesn't want to involve the police, at least not yet."

Harry nodded. "Do you want me to make some inquiries?"

"No, but thank you. My friend has agreed to speak to the police in another few days if she doesn't hear from Erica."

THE CARTER FILE

"From where has she gone missing?"

"Liverpool."

"I have some connections there. Please let me know if I can help."

"I appreciate the offer. As I said, my friend isn't convinced that there's actually anything wrong. Not yet, anyway."

"Here we are," the waiter announced, putting plates full of food on the table in front of them. "Anything else?"

"No, thank you," Bessie said, eyeing up her chicken and leek pie. "This looks delicious."

The man nodded and walked away, leaving Bessie and Harry to their lunch.

"It's very good," Harry said, sounding almost surprised.

"Save room for pudding," Bessie advised. "The puddings are as good as the meals."

"I rarely eat pudding."

"Why?"

Harry blinked several times, staring at Bessie. "Because too much sugar isn't healthy," he said eventually.

Bessie shrugged. "Having a pudding now and again isn't going to ruin my health," she said. "And it does wonders for my mental health, too. Pudding makes me happy."

"For a short while, anyway," Harry suggested.

"I've learned over my years to take every bit of happiness I can get. The moments can sometimes seem to be quite far apart, really."

"I suppose so."

"What makes you happy?" Bessie asked.

Harry stared at her and then slowly took a bite of his lunch. He chewed and swallowed, and then washed the steak and kidney pie down with some tea before he spoke. "No idea," he said.

"What do you mean by that?"

"I don't give happiness much thought."

"Maybe you should."

"Solving murders makes me feel as if my life has purpose, anyway," he said after another long pause. "There's something very satisfying about getting justice for an innocent victim, or even a not-so-innocent one."

"Should we talk about murder, then?" Bessie asked.

The crashing noise behind her made her jump. The waiter was standing behind her, staring at the tray he'd just dropped. It had been full of dirty crockery, most of which had shattered when it had hit the floor.

"I'm so sorry," he said as another waiter rushed over. The pair of them cleared away the mess as quickly as they could.

When Bessie turned back around, Harry looked amused. "I should have warned you that he was behind you. Murder can be a sensitive subject."

"Maybe we should save the conversation for after lunch, then," Bessie suggested.

"I suspect we'll be left alone for some time now," Harry told her. "Let's talk about murder."

CHAPTER 11

"I don't even know where to begin," Bessie said.

"You seem to suspect Harvey."

"I don't know that I suspect him so much as dislike him," Bessie countered. "He simply doesn't seem likeable, but that doesn't mean he's a killer. He may just be an unpleasant person."

"So who killed Julie Carter?"

Bessie sighed. "That's the problem. I have no idea. I read the recent interviews last night and looked back through them this morning, and I still don't feel any closer to understanding what happened in that cabin than I was when we first started talking about the case."

"Which is often the case with investigations."

"Is it? That really hasn't been my experience. Maybe it's the lack of motive that's bothering me. I don't care for Harvey, but I can't imagine why he'd want to kill Julie, unless he'd made a play for her and she'd turned him down. We need to understand his relationship with Mary Ellen better."

"We need to understand all of the relationships better.

Asking the police to find an outside witness who knew all of the suspects at the time was very clever."

"I hope so. I think asking them to create their own timelines could be helpful, if they can remember enough."

"I suspect some of them will never forget that weekend," Harry said. "The killer, most obviously."

"So if one of them comes back with a very detailed timeline, he or she should be moved up the list of suspects?"

"Maybe. He or she may be smart enough to pretend to have forgotten a lot of the details, though, as well. He or she has been getting away with murder for fifteen years, after all."

"So who do you think did it?" Bessie had to ask.

"I have Mary Ellen and Jack at the top of my list because they were the most changed by the event, but Mike also has a top spot. He's the only one with a motive and without even a weak alibi. Of course, if it were that simple, he would have been charged fifteen years ago."

Bessie nodded. "He does seem the most obvious suspect."

"And yet he was never arrested, never charged, apparently not even questioned more thoroughly than any of the others. I should have had Andrew ask his police colleague in Pennsylvania about that, actually."

"I can mention it to him later today," Bessie offered.

He shrugged. "I'll be sending him an email this afternoon summarising all of my thoughts on the case. I'll mention it to him in that email."

"So if those three are at the top of your list, Harvey and Katie are at the bottom?" Bessie asked as she scooped up her last bite of pie.

He nodded. "I don't care for Harvey any more than you do, but I don't think he killed Julie. Having said that, if someone came up with a credible motive for him, I could be easily persuaded to change my mind."

"And Katie?" Bessie asked as Harry stopped to finish his own meal.

"I can't imagine any motive for her. She seemed to have been overwhelmed by the entire experience of the weekend, even before the murder. Of course, she found the body, as well. Sometimes killers will make sure to be the ones who find the bodies in order to make sure they have control over the situation, but that definitely doesn't seem to have been the case here."

"According to her statement, she walked into the room, spotted the body, and then got hysterical."

"And the others all agreed. Jack said he'd come running when he'd heard her screaming and found her on the ground, shrieking and crying and terrified."

"Finding a body is a scary experience."

"I understand you've found quite a few in the past three years."

"I have."

"And have you ever started shrieking and crying when you've found one?"

"No, but I've also never found a friend's body in the same cabin where I was staying during what was meant to be a celebration weekend," Bessie told him. "I'm also a few years older than eighteen."

"Katie's reaction could have been a deliberate attempt to hide the fact that she'd killed Julie, but having read all of the accounts of her hysteria, I'm inclined to believe that it was genuine and that she didn't have anything to do with Julie's death."

Bessie nodded. "I'd definitely put her at the bottom of my list of suspects."

"Give me your list, then," Harry challenged her.

"I'll have to think for a moment," she replied.

"And here's the waiter," Harry said in a low voice a second later.

"Pudding menus?" the waiter asked.

"Yes, please," Bessie replied.

Harry shook his head. "Nothing for me."

Bessie waited until the waiter had taken her order for Victoria sponge before she replied to Harry. "Do warn me when he comes back with my pudding," she said.

He nodded. "Do you have your list in order, then?"

"In spite of everything you've said, I still want Harvey at the top of my list," she admitted. "I suppose Mike has to be second on the list, as he had a motive and the best opportunity, but he seemed far more likeable than Harvey, and he seemed genuinely distraught over the murder."

"I agree with you about that. He said quite touching things about Julie in his recent interview."

"He sounded sincere, too. I do find that aspect of the cold case unit incredibly frustrating."

"Not getting to interview the witnesses or suspects yourself?"

Flushing, Bessie nodded. "I've never been able to actually interview anyone myself, of course, but I do feel that I learn a lot from talking to people myself rather than through all of these intermediaries."

"I've been doing consulting work for so long that I've become quite accustomed to the process," Harry told her. "It's been a great many years since I conducted an interview of my own."

"You don't miss it?"

"I do miss it, but I also enjoy being one step removed. While I miss out on seeing expressions and hearing tones of voice, it's sometimes easier to see the bigger picture when you're on the outside. I'm also finding that I'm enjoying working in a team. I wasn't expecting that."

"I can't imagine working any other way."

"And here's your pudding," Harry told her, nodding at the waiter who was hovering behind Bessie.

The man put the plate down in front of Bessie and then rushed away.

"Let's finish your list. Harvey, then Mike, then who?" Harry asked as Bessie picked up her fork.

"Jack, maybe." Bessie sighed. "I hate to say that a woman wouldn't stab another woman, but I can't help but feel as if a man is more likely to have been the killer than a woman."

"So Mary Ellen fourth and Katie last?" Harry asked.

Bessie nodded. "We agree on the least likely suspect, anyway."

Harry grinned. "Maybe I should tell Andrew to have the police focus on Katie. Maybe we're both badly wrong."

"If you had to put one person on the top of your list, which one would it be? You had Mary Ellen and Jack both at the top, didn't you?"

"I did. I suppose I'd put Jack at the top, although by only the smallest of margins. Then Mary Ellen and then Mike."

"What possible motive could any of them had?" Bessie asked.

"Any of the men could have made a play for her and been rejected," Harry suggested.

"I suppose either of the women could have done the same."

Harry raised an eyebrow. "You're right, of course, although we've no evidence to suggest that any of the women were so inclined."

"So maybe one of the men made a play for Julie and wasn't rejected," Bessie said. "Maybe that man's girlfriend found out."

"That seems the most likely explanation if the killer was one of the women."

Bessie sighed. "They'd finished high school, and none of them were going to the same college. I can't see there being any motives tied up in their future plans, can you?"

"Not unless there was more to their future plans that we've been told."

"Julie was going to California," Bessie recalled. "Why would someone kill her when she was going to be leaving soon anyway?"

"Maybe Mike wanted her to go to the same college that he was planning to attend."

"And when she wouldn't, he killed her? That seems a strange motive."

"Maybe I'm grasping at straws," Harry said. "Really, the only motive that makes any sense, based on what we know so far, anyway, has to be something to do with Julie being involved with one of the other men, or one of the other men wanting to be involved with her."

"Unless Mike killed her over whatever they fought about," Bessie said. She washed her last bite of cake down with the last of her tea. "Delicious," she said.

"I'm glad you enjoyed it. Should we head back to Laxey now, or are there other wonderful sites to see in Peel?"

"The castle is worth a visit, but it's closed for the season at the moment."

He frowned. "That's disappointing."

Bessie glanced at the window. The heavy rain from the morning was still falling. "It's mostly in ruins. You really wouldn't want to walk around the site today."

He shrugged. "So back to Laxey?"

"The museum in Douglas is very good," Bessie told him. "By the time we drive there, though, we'd struggle to get through it all before they close for the day."

"Let's leave that for another day then. I hope you won't mind being my tour guide another time."

"Not at all. I always enjoy visiting the island's heritage sites, and I welcome the chance to share the island's history with visitors."

"And we don't always have to talk about murder," he teased as he got to his feet.

"I suspect we always will, though," Bessie replied.

They walked back to his car, talking about the weather. It didn't take Harry long to drive her back to Treoghe Bwaane.

"Thank you for an interesting morning," he told her as he walked her to the cottage's door. "I'll see you tomorrow at two."

"See you tomorrow," Bessie repeated before she opened her door and went inside.

The conversation over lunch had left Bessie feeling restless and a bit frustrated. She found herself feeling as if she wasn't getting anywhere with the case. Pulling out all of the police reports she'd been given, along with the notes she'd taken at the meetings, she began at the beginning again, carefully rereading everything.

Two hours later, she had a headache. "I'm not any closer to a solution," she told her mirror image as she opened the bottle of headache tablets. "I need to know more about the young people and their relationships with one another. That has to be the key to the murder."

As she walked back to the kitchen, she shook her head. "Maybe I need to stop talking to myself, as well," she muttered.

Someone knocked as she was staring into the refrigerator, wondering what to prepare for dinner.

"I hope you haven't had dinner yet," Andrew said as a greeting. "I've just spent an incredibly long day trying to find a compromise that everyone in the family can live with and, at the moment, I don't even know if I've managed it. I didn't get lunch, and I'm hungrier than I've been in a very long time."

"I can have something ready in thirty minutes," Bessie offered.

Andrew shook his head. "Let's go into Douglas, to that Italian restaurant right on the promenade. Once we get there, they'll have garlic bread to us within minutes of ordering. A few slices of garlic bread will improve my mood immensely."

Bessie grinned. "Give me two minutes to get ready," she said, heading for the stairs.

"No more than two," he called after her.

They were on their way to Douglas a short while later. As Andrew drove, Bessie told him about the conversation she and Harry had had over lunch.

"I've had a long email back from the detective in Pennsylvania," he told her. "One of his colleagues at the station actually went to school with Julie and the others. He's going to sit down tonight and write out everything he can remember about the six men and women who were at the cabin. I should have the report tomorrow."

"Let's just hope it helps," Bessie replied. "What about asking them all for timelines?"

"He's giving the idea some thought," Andrew said, sounding frustrated. "I got the impression that he doesn't want to go back and speak to everyone again so soon after the last round of interviews. I think he's going to wait until we've given him quite a long list of things to ask them all before he revisits them."

"He didn't actually interview most of them, though," Bessie said, thinking about the names of the various police officers she'd seen on the reports.

"No, he sent requests to officers in each person's local jurisdiction. That may be part of why he's reluctant to go back to them again, as well. Coordinating that effort probably took him a lot of time."

"But Julie was murdered," Bessie said quietly.

Andrew nodded. "I'm hoping the information we get from the officer who knew them fifteen years ago will be helpful. Right now, I don't feel as if we're really getting anywhere on this case."

He parked in one of the car parks near the centre of Douglas, and then he and Bessie made their way to the restaurant. They were seated almost immediately, and Bessie ordered the garlic bread before anything else.

Andrew ate his first slice before he even opened his menu. Once they'd ordered, he sat back and slowly ate a second.

"I feel better now," he said as he reached for a third.

Bessie nodded. "I hope things aren't too bad at home."

"They aren't bad, exactly, just complicated," he sighed. "Parents make plans for their children, and then their children insist on having minds of their own. As I said, I spent the day putting together a compromise, but no one has actually agreed to it yet. I'll probably be busy again tomorrow morning trying to convince everyone that my compromise is the best option. I'm actually rather hoping that someone else comes up with a better plan, but I don't see that happening."

They talked about British politics and world affairs while they ate pasta and garlic bread. Andrew insisted that they order pudding, so Bessie had a slice of tiramisu, even though she was already quite full. It was dark and rainy when they left the restaurant.

"I was going to suggest a long drive around the island," Andrew said, looking up at the cloudy skies.

"This isn't the best weather for enjoying the island's views."

"No, maybe we should go back to Laxey and open a bottle of wine instead."

Bessie didn't drink often, but at the moment, the idea appealed to her. "I'm not certain what type of biscuits go best with wine, but I have several varieties in the cupboard."

Half an hour later, they were sipping wine and eating biscuits in Bessie's cosy sitting room.

"Have you managed to find Grace's friend yet?" Andrew asked.

Bessie sighed and shook her head. "I meant to ring her and tell her that I've not had any luck. Grace suggested that I try speaking to her former boyfriend, and I happened to meet him today in Peel. Unfortunately, he claimed that he hadn't spoken to Erica in months."

"He claimed? Did you doubt him?"

"No, not at all. If he was lying, he's very good at it."

"Are you ready to involve the police, then?"

"I'm going to go and see Grace in the morning," Bessie said, surprising herself. "She said she'd ring the police if she hadn't heard anything by Wednesday, but I'm hoping to persuade her to do something tomorrow."

"I have a friend in Liverpool who would probably be happy to help. He's retired now, and I know he's bored. Of course, we have Charles, as well. He's one of the country's leading experts in missing persons."

"Let me see what Grace says. I'll let you know."

Between them, they finished the bottle of wine and ate far too many biscuits. It was getting late, by Bessie's standards, anyway, when Andrew finally got up, ready to head back to his cottage.

"Thank you for spending the evening with me," he told Bessie. "I've had my mobile switched off all night. No doubt I have a dozen or more messages to deal with, but it was lovely to forget all about my family for a few hours."

Bessie gave him a hug. "I'm sorry," she said.

"I'm not. As much as they make me crazy, I love them all, and I wouldn't trade them for anything. I'm probably going to be busy all morning with them, but maybe we could get lunch again on our way to the meeting. Somewhere other than the Seaview, perhaps?"

"I'd like that."

"Be ready for midday. I'll ring you or text you if anything changes."

As Bessie crawled into bed, she glanced at the clock. *I could sleep until seven tomorrow,* she thought. *That would give me something close to the amount of sleep I normally get, anyway.*

HER EYES OPENED at three minutes past six. Frowning, she rolled over and tried to get back to sleep. Only a minute later, she gave up and got out of bed. Vaguely aware that she'd had nightmares about being chased by men with knives, she let the shower wash the memories away. As she patted on the rose-scented dusting powder that was her daily reminder of Matthew, she wondered idly what he would think of how her life had turned out.

When she'd known him, she'd thought she wanted to marry him and start a family. Her life with Matthew would have looked very different to the life she'd actually led. Now she couldn't imagine being a wife and a mother. As she got dressed, she shook her head to clear away the memories and thoughts that were filling her head. She needed to focus on the day ahead, talking with Grace and then, later, meeting with the cold case unit.

Breakfast was cereal with milk and a cup of yoghurt. As she headed for the door, she grabbed an apple out of the fruit bowl on the table to eat while she walked. The skies were overcast and grey, but it was dry.

Walking to the water's edge, Bessie turned and began a brisk walk across the sand. It wasn't long before she was past the holiday cottages. The stairs to Thie yn Traie were next, and Bessie found herself glancing up at them as she walked, wondering how Elizabeth was doing with restarting her party planning business.

The rain began as the new houses came into sight. Bessie increased her pace, trying not to stare at the backs of the homes. The curtains were tightly drawn in nearly every window anyway, and Bessie began to worry that Grace would be either out or still in bed. As the rain became heavier, she hurried towards the back of the Wattersons' house, hoping to see some lights on inside.

"Bessie, hurry," Grace called as she suddenly appeared at the back of her house, having pulled open the curtains and then slid open the sliding doors.

A moment later, Bessie was standing in the house's sitting room, dripping water all over the floor.

CHAPTER 12

"I'm going to ruin your floors," Bessie said apologetically.

"That section is tile, so it can get wet and covered in sand," Grace assured her. "Hugh and I were talking about redoing all of the floors on the ground floor in tile, actually. We both love living right on the beach, but sand does get everywhere."

Bessie nodded. "It truly does."

Grace brought Bessie a bath sheet, and Bessie wrapped herself up and then sighed. "I wasn't expecting the rain."

"I'm just glad I opened the curtains when I did. If I'd have been a few minutes later, you would have thought I wasn't home."

"And I'd have been completely soaked by the time I'd have made it back to Treoghe Bwaane."

"As it is, Aalish and I will have to give you a ride home. You can't walk in that rain."

Bessie wanted to argue. She hated feeling as if she were taking advantage of her friends, but she also hated the thought of walking home in heavy rain and, at the moment at least, the rain didn't appear as if it were going to stop. "We'll see," was all that she would concede at the moment.

"How are you, aside from wet?" Grace asked.

"I'm fine, but I'm worried about your friend Erica. I think you need to get the police involved."

"Tomorrow. Tomorrow makes it a week since I sent the first text message to which she hasn't replied."

"I actually bumped into Ian Branson yesterday. He said he hasn't spoken to Erica in months."

"Where did you find him?"

Bessie told the girl the whole story. When she was done, Grace sighed.

"I was really hoping that he'd spoken to her in the last day or two," she said. "I'm still not ready to ring the police, but I'm slightly more worried."

"Can you think of anyone else to ring?" Bessie asked. "Do you know anyone that she knows in Liverpool, for instance?"

Grace shook her head. "I've spoken to everyone I know who used to work with her when she was teaching. None of the others have kept in touch, at least not regularly. I've also left two more messages on her voicemail, but I feel odd about doing that. As I said before, the last time she went missing she was with a man."

"What man?"

Grace blinked and then shrugged. "I'm not sure she ever told me his name," she said slowly. "This was about six months ago now. I kept ringing and texting while she and the new man in her life were off having fun together."

"And is she still involved with him?"

"Oh, no. I thought I told you that she was single. That relationship didn't last very long at all. Erica is really good at meeting men and starting new relationships, but they never seem to last very long."

"Any idea why?"

"Erica has a short attention span," Grace told her with a rueful grin. "She gets tired of men very quickly, even quite nice men who treat her well."

"I don't know what else I can do," Bessie said. "I really think this is a police matter now."

Grace nodded, but when she opened her mouth, a loud crying noise filled the air. "And that's my daughter," Grace laughed, nodding towards the baby monitor on the counter. "I'd better go and get her."

"Hello," Bessie said to Aalish as Grace carried her into the room.

Aalish stared at her for a moment and then replied in a long stream of babble.

"Are you quite certain?" Bessie asked.

Another long reply that ended with a high-pitched squeal made Bessie and Grace both laugh.

"She does enjoy having conversations now," Grace told Bessie. "I just wish I could understand what she's saying."

"I'm sure it won't be long before she's talking."

"No doubt, and then I'll probably want her to stop."

"But we were talking about you getting the police involved in the search for Erica."

"Yes, I know, and I will, tomorrow," Grace said. "For now, I should take you home, though. Aalish and I are supposed to be going to visit a friend this morning. We can drop you off on our way out."

"I don't want to inconvenience you."

"It's no inconvenience. I appreciate everything you've done to help, really."

"I'll ring the bank again later this morning," Bessie promised once they were all in the car heading towards Treoghe Bwaane. "I'll let you know if I learn anything."

"Thank you," Grace said. "I really hope she turns up today or tomorrow so that I don't have to report her missing."

"Me too."

As soon as she got inside, Bessie rang the bank and asked for Erica.

"I'm sorry, but Ms. Tucker isn't going to be in today. I can connect you to someone else who can help or to Ms. Tucker's voicemail," the woman on the other end offered.

"I'll leave a message on voicemail," Bessie said impulsively.

"This is Erica Tucker in the lending department. Please leave your message after the tone. I'll ring you back at my earliest convenience."

"Ah, yes, Ms. Tucker, my name is Bessie Cubbon. I've been thinking about buying an investment property in Liverpool, and a friend of mine gave me your name. Please ring me back." Bessie carefully stated her telephone number and then put the phone down. While she was tempted to work on Carree's diaries, she found herself going back through the Carter case file yet again, convinced that she must have missed something.

"The police didn't ask nearly enough questions fifteen years ago," she complained to Andrew as they drove into Ramsey just after midday. "I know that Harvey and Mary Ellen had lawyers sitting with them, but the police seemed to have been very careful about what they asked all five of the suspects."

Andrew nodded. "It's a small town, and the young men and women involved belonged to some of the town's most important families. I think they felt as if they had to be very careful. Having said that, a lot of the information that we're seeking is information that the local police may have had but not bothered to note, such as the relationships between the young people. Maybe everyone in Greenview knew that Harvey and Mary Ellen had been together for years, but that Harvey cheated on her constantly, for example. The police may not have added that information to their notes because it was common knowledge."

"I can't see that sort of thing being common knowledge," Bessie said thoughtfully. "They were high school students, after all. Maybe if Harvey's mother were cheating, that would have been known throughout the town, but were the men and women in Greenview interested in what the high school students were doing?"

"I don't know. Light and Baxter was the only law firm in town. Would that make their children's lives of interest to anyone?"

Bessie shrugged. "I don't pay attention to what my advocate's children are doing — well, aside from the children who study law and come to work with my advocate."

"And Harvey and Mary Ellen were expected to do just that, so maybe people kept an eye on them."

"Maybe," Bessie replied, not convinced. "Or maybe the original investigation was done badly."

Andrew laughed. "That's also a possibility. Certainly, things were missed that I would have included if I'd been the one conducting the investigation, but again, it's a small town, and the police there don't often deal with murder investigations. I suppose it isn't surprising that things were missed."

He pulled into the car park for a small café near the centre of Ramsey. "Did I find the right place?" he asked.

Bessie nodded. She'd recommended the café because they had a nice menu with some variety. The last time she'd eaten there, the food had been very good, as well. Assuming they still had the same staff in the kitchen, she was sure they'd have a good lunch.

"That was nice," Andrew told her an hour later as they walked back to his car.

"Just nice?"

He shrugged. "Everything was fine, but nothing was incredible."

Bessie nodded. "I'm afraid I have to agree. I was a bit disappointed in the sticky toffee pudding, as well. They were a bit stingy with the sauce."

"Never mind. Maybe Jasper has done something nice for us for the meeting."

The drive to the Seaview took only a few minutes. Jasper was in the foyer, talking with the man behind the desk, when they arrived.

"Ah, Bessie, Andrew, hello," he said brightly as he turned towards them. "Good afternoon. I've put you in the penthouse again. They're probably still setting up the catering. Let's go and see, shall we?"

He led them to the lifts and pressed the button. "Someone needs to have a word with young Andy Caine," Jasper said to Bessie in a low voice as they boarded the car.

"What's wrong?" Bessie asked.

"We don't mind a bit of competition, but when a restaurant has signature items on the menu, it's out of order for another chef to blatantly copy those items and offer them on a catering basis," he replied.

"Andy did that?"

"Jennifer Johnson is giving out a new catering menu to prospective clients. One of them rang me when he saw what was on the menu because he was confused to see items from our dinner menu on her catering menu. The descriptions on her menu are very close to the ones on ours, and she hasn't even bothered to rename the dishes. My friend thought that the chef from here was doing the catering, but of course, he is not."

"My goodness," Bessie exclaimed. The lift doors opened and Bessie followed Jasper and Andrew down the corridor, her mind racing.

"I rang Jennifer to protest, and she laughed and told me that everything on the menu had come from Andy Caine, and that I would have to take up any complaints with him," Jasper added.

"I'll speak to him," Bessie promised, making a mental note to ring him as soon as she was home from the meeting.

"I don't have any sort of relationship with Andy," Jasper told her. "I don't want to ring him out of the blue to demand that he make changes to his menu, but he needs to understand how things are done on a small island where people do better when they work together than at odds with one another."

He opened the door to the conference room and led them inside. Three members of the catering team were setting up at the back of the room.

"I did finger sandwiches and a selection of puddings," Jasper told them. "Chef is trying out some new recipes, so you have three or four of each pudding, each done to a slightly different recipe."

"Did you want us to tell you which ones we prefer?" Bessie asked.

"That won't be necessary. Chef will have tried each of the options, and he'll make his own decisions as to which is best. I've given up trying to persuade him that the opinion of anyone else matters," Jasper replied.

Bessie laughed. "So we'll just enjoy everything."

"To be fair, I doubt you'll notice much difference in the various options. He makes only tiny changes each time, and his choices often have as much to do with ease of preparation and appearance than they do taste," Jasper added.

Bessie filled a plate with sandwiches and small pieces of various puddings. She laughed when she saw the sticky toffee pudding. A bowl full of toffee sauce was sitting next to the cake pieces.

"You can have as much as you want," Andrew told Bessie.

"Toffee sauce isn't a beverage," she muttered under her breath as she added a few pieces of the cake to her plate before covering them in sauce.

They were sitting at the table, chatting about the food, when John and Doona arrived. Hugh wasn't far behind, and Charles and Harry arrived together while Hugh was still filling his plate.

"I hope you have something interesting to tell us," Harry said once everyone was at the table. "This case doesn't seem to be going anywhere at the moment."

"I did warn all of you when we started that we were very unlikely to be able to solve more than one or two cases a year," Andrew reminded him. "We've already solved two and we're only on our third case."

"And this is where our streak ends," Charles said.

"Not necessarily. I've had a long statement from a young police officer who was at school with Julie and the others. He was able to provide a lot of good background information," Andrew told him.

"He wasn't questioned when Julie died?" Doona asked.

"There was something in the original reports about the entire senior class, all one hundred and six of them, being interviewed, but that nothing interesting was learned," John remembered.

"I have asked the detective in Pennsylvania if anyone kept copies of those interviews. He's going to check, but he doesn't believe they bothered. According to him, all of the kids expressed shock that someone had murdered Julie and that none of them could believe that the killer was one of the other five people who were in the cabin with her. I'd like to believe that we'd find a lot of interesting information in those interviews, but sadly, I don't believe they still exist," Andrew told him.

"But the statement you got is from a police officer?" Bessie asked.

"Yes, and that's quite interesting, too," Andrew replied. "Does anyone have any questions or comments about the case before I start reading this statement to you? I'm going to give you all copies, of course, but I want to read it out to you, slowly, so that we can discuss some of the key points."

"No questions," Harry snapped, clearly eager to hear the statement.

The others all shrugged or shook their heads. After a moment, Andrew held up several sheets of paper that had been stapled together. "I'm going to paraphrase a great deal, rather than read it word for word. As I said, you'll have copies when you leave today."

"This better be good," Harry muttered.

"The young man's name is Robbie Masters," Andrew told them. "Robbie graduated in the same class as the six men and women who were celebrating at the cabin. Up until graduation, he'd been planning to go to college to become an accountant. His mother is an accountant. His parents divorced when he was a child, and his father moved away from Greenview. I don't believe his father was in his life, at least not much."

"Is all of this background necessary?" Harry asked. "I mean, we all know Robbie didn't kill Julie."

"Sorry, I found the background fascinating," Andrew told him. "You may agree when I tell you that Robbie and Julie were a couple, somewhat briefly, about a year before Julie's death."

"That is interesting," Harry admitted. "I assume Robbie wasn't in the same social circle as Harvey and Mary Ellen."

"He was not. Julie was on the periphery of that circle, but because of her mother's issues, she was not really a member of the popular crowd. At least, that's how Robbie saw it. As he put it, he'd had a crush on her since middle school, but hadn't worked up the nerve to ask her out until the end of junior year, which was, as I said, about a year before graduation," Andrew replied.

"It didn't last long?" Bessie asked.

"The relationship started when Julie asked him to tutor her in math for a few weeks before the final exam at the end of the school year," Andrew explained. "He says they were two weeks into the tutoring before he finally asked her out on a date. They went out for about two weeks after that, until after the school year finished. Then Julie went away for the summer to some camp in California. When she came back, she told him she wasn't interested in restarting their relationship."

"And the poor kid had probably spent the whole summer waiting for her," Hugh guessed.

"He had, yes," Andrew replied. "And then he spent all of senior year watching her from afar. When she was killed, Robbie decided that he wanted to become a police officer so that he could get justice for Julie."

"If he knows anything relevant, why didn't he share it with the police years ago?" Doona demanded. "If he wants justice that badly, I mean."

"He clearly doesn't think he knows anything relevant," Andrew told her. "He says in his statement that everything he's put in it he also told the police at the time."

"So we have to hope that we spot something they missed," Hugh suggested.

"We're coming at it from a very different angle," Andrew said. "We don't know any of the people involved, so we're trying to understand the different relationships. I believe the police at the time thought they knew about and understood the relationships."

"So what did he have to say about the six people in the cabin that weekend?" Doona asked.

"Harvey and Mary Ellen were the kids that everyone wanted to be," Andrew told her. "They had money and cars, and they were allowed to pretty much do whatever they wanted. By that, I mean they drank underage and had parties at their parents' houses, and they decided who was invited to all of the social events that really mattered."

"They, as in they always did everything together?" Bessie checked.

"They'd been a couple since middle school," Andrew told her. "Robbie remembered only one occasion when the pair had broken up in all those years. It was in the spring of senior year. According to Robbie, they had a huge fight and were apart for about two months, most of March and April and into May, according to Robbie. Except then it was time for prom, which is the biggest high school social event of the year, so they got back together."

"We need to find out more about those two months," Bessie said.

"Let me finish telling you what Robbie said about everyone," Andrew replied. "He didn't care for Harvey and he thought Mary Ellen was a snob who really only appreciated money. He didn't think she cared at all for Harvey, that she simply found him useful."

"Ouch," Doona said.

Andrew nodded. "He had nicer things to say about Jack Morton, whose family lived near where Robbie and his mother lived. They were friendly, if not exactly friends. He thought Katie was sweet, and he admitted to being slightly disappointed when she'd started seeing Jack and spending time with the popular crowd. I got the feeling that he'd been hoping to ask her out, but then she and Jack got together and he didn't get the chance."

"That just leaves Mike and Julie," Bessie said as Andrew paused for a drink.

"He didn't really care for Mike, although he admitted that he barely knew him. Mike didn't take a lot of math or science classes, and Robbie didn't take much else, apparently. As for Julie, he was crazy about her, and he was really sad when she got involved with Mike," Andrew said.

"Did he say how they happened to start seeing one another?" Doona asked.

"He did, and that's where it gets interesting," Andrew replied. "Julie started spending time with the popular crowd when she started seeing Harvey during those two months when he and Mary Ellen weren't together."

Bessie felt her jaw drop. "Why wasn't that mentioned in any of the interviews?" she demanded.

"No one seemed to think it was significant," Andrew replied. "I asked the detective who'd done the initial investigation, and he said that they hadn't bothered themselves too much with worrying about short-lived teenaged romances. According to him, just about everyone at the cabin had been involved with just about everyone else at some point during their high school years."

Bessie frowned. "If that's true, there may have been quite a few people in the cabin with a motive for murder."

CHAPTER 13

"But is it true?" Harry demanded. "What did Robbie say about that?"

"Again, let's start with Harvey and Mary Ellen. Aside from that one two-month stretch, they were a couple all through school. During the two months they were apart, it seems as if Harvey went out with just about every other girl in the school, not just Julie. Robbie reckons that Harvey and Julie were together for no more than a week, maybe less. He also thought that Julie was one of the first girls that Harvey took out after he and Mary Ellen split. She was already seeing Mike by the time Harvey and Mary Ellen got back together."

"What about Katie?" John asked. "Did Harvey go out with Katie during his time apart from Mary Ellen?"

"No, Katie and Jack were already a couple when Harvey and Mary Ellen split," Andrew told him. "At least, that's how Robbie remembers it."

"And with whom was Mary Ellen involved during those two months?" Bessie asked.

"Robbie didn't think she'd been involved with anyone. He

said she seemed to be enjoying being on her own. He even thought about asking her out himself, because she started hanging out in the library once in a while and seemed to be working harder on her schoolwork rather than drinking and partying all the time," Andrew replied.

"And then she got back together with Harvey," John said.

"She did, and according to Robbie, she went right back to drinking and partying and skipping school," Andrew told him.

"What about the others? Did Julie ever go out with Jack, or had Katie and Mike ever been a couple?" Doona wondered.

Andrew shook his head. "Robbie wasn't certain about Katie, but he was adamant that Julie never went out with Jack. He seems to have kept a close eye on her, especially during their last year of school."

"But he wasn't certain about Katie and Mike?" Bessie checked.

"Not completely certain, but he didn't remember hearing their names being linked. Apparently, gossip about who was seeing whom was the main topic of conversation at the school in between classes. Robbie said he knew more about his classmates' love lives than he'd ever wanted to know," Andrew said.

"What else did he have to say?" Bessie asked.

"Not a lot. We'd specifically asked about the relationships between the young people, so that's what he addressed. I can, of course, ask him for more information about anything," Andrew replied.

"Did he ever hear anything about the fight between Mike and Julie?" Bessie asked as the thought crossed her mind.

"He did not. He also didn't know why Harvey and Mary Ellen split up. He said it was odd because such things were usually widely discussed, but that if anyone could keep secrets, it was Harvey and his friends," Andrew told them.

"I think the temporary split between Harvey and Mary Ellen is significant," Bessie said. "It may well give both Harvey and Mary Ellen motives for Julie's murder."

"You think they fought about Julie?" Harry asked.

"Maybe, or maybe the fight isn't important but what happened next is. Maybe Harvey really fell for Julie and she wasn't interested. Maybe he was still mad about it four months later," Bessie suggested.

"Or maybe Harvey dumped Mary Ellen because he wanted to go out with Julie, and Mary Ellen was still mad about it four months later," Harry countered.

Bessie shrugged. "You have your favourite suspect and I have mine," she said.

Harry nodded. "I think someone needs to ask both Mary Ellen and Harvey about that break-up," he told Andrew. "If I were a betting man, I'd bet that they'll both insist that they don't remember what it was about, not after all this time. They'll both be lying, as well."

Andrew nodded. "I agree. It may have just been a high school romance, but they'd been together for a long time, and they got back together after a short break. I'm certain they both remember every detail, but I can see them both claiming otherwise."

"They'll be especially quick to pretend to have forgotten if their time apart was tied in any way to the murder," John said.

"I'm going to request that both Harvey and Mary Ellen be interviewed again. I want them both asked about the fight and their months apart and about the fight between Mike and Julie. I'd like them both to be asked to attempt to put together a timeline for the weekend. We'll see if we get any results from any of that," Andrew said.

"I think we will," Harry said. "I think things are finally moving in the right direction on this case."

Andrew nodded. "I agree. At the time of the murder, of course, both Mary Ellen and Harvey had their lawyers sitting with them during questioning. I'd hate to think that the police skirted around any difficult questions because of that."

"It's possible the police truly didn't think the various romances mattered. It's also possible that they didn't," John said. "This feels significant because it's the first we've heard about it, but the police at the time may have known all about it and simply disregarded it as irrelevant."

"Let's meet again on Thursday," Andrew said. "I don't know if that's enough time for me to have heard back from Pennsylvania or not, considering they'll have to arrange for Mary Ellen's interview in Colorado, but we can talk about whatever Harvey had to say, assuming his interview has been done by that time."

Andrew passed around copies of the interview with Robbie Masters and then sat back down. Bessie finished everything on her plate as the room slowly cleared.

"Even Charles appeared slightly more optimistic when he left," Bessie said as the door shut behind John and Doona.

Andrew laughed. "He did. I think we're all feeling the same way, as if we've found the key to the whole case, but we may be completely wrong."

"We've found a key, and hopefully it will open a door or a window to more information," Bessie said. "Every scrap of information moves us closer to the solution."

"I can't quite work out why this case was never solved," Andrew said as he got to his feet. "They had only five suspects to consider."

"Maybe because all five of them seem both equally likely and equally unlikely. They all had the means and the opportunity, after all, and we've no real idea what the motive might have been. Aside from the fight with Mike, no one has suggested any reason why anyone would have wanted Julie dead."

"Unless it was something to do with the fight between Mary Ellen and Harvey back in March," Andrew said. "That's the first really interesting thing we've learned since we started."

"I can see the five of them all covering for one another back when the murder first happened," Bessie said thoughtfully. "Actually, I can't, really. I can't imagine covering up for a murderer, but I suppose I can see the young people in a small town doing so. I still think someone knows something, though, and I can't understand why he or she hasn't come forward now, after all these years. It isn't as if they're all still friends."

"That's another question for the police to put to Mary Ellen and Harvey," Andrew said, making a quick note. "Which of the five of them are still in contact with the others? From their recent interviews, it didn't sound as if any of them had stayed in touch, but the question was never specifically asked."

"I wouldn't blame them for not wanting to stay in touch. I suspect they all want to forget about that weekend."

Andrew nodded. "Let's head back to Laxey. I want to get this email sent as quickly as possible to maximize the chance of having a reply by Thursday."

"And I need to ring Andy," Bessie said, mostly to remind herself.

"Shall we go somewhere for dinner later?" Andrew asked as he parked outside Bessie's cottage.

"We could, or I could cook something."

"Let's go out. What about the restaurant that you told me about that does the small plates of different foods? Didn't you say they were open in their new location?"

Bessie smiled. Dan and Carol Jenkins had originally opened their restaurant in the small neighbouring village of Lonan. When it had proven to be a huge success, they'd decided to relocate to a larger facility. The process had taken a good deal longer than anyone had anticipated, but the new restaurant had hosted a grand opening a few weeks earlier. Bessie had been thrilled to have been invited to the opening, and she felt terrible that she hadn't been back since. "Yes, let's go there," she said quickly.

"I'll collect you around half five," he told her.

Inside her cottage, Bessie grabbed the phone.

"Hello?"

"Anne? It's Bessie. I need to speak to Andy," Bessie told Andy's mother, who was a close friend of hers.

"I'm sorry, but he isn't here. He's never here any longer. He's far too busy elsewhere. I'll leave him a note that you rang, but don't be surprised if he doesn't ring you back. He's, well, he's not himself right now."

"Yes, so I've heard," Bessie said. "Jasper at the Seaview is very upset that Andy is putting menu items from the Seaview's restaurant on the catering menu for Jennifer's events."

Anne sighed deeply. "No doubt it's all Jennifer's doing, but she'll be more than happy to let everyone think Andy's behind it. I've tried my best, but I don't care for the girl, and I really don't want her to marry my son."

"Please ask Andy to ring me back. You might even tell him that it's important," Bessie said.

"I'll tell him, or rather, I'll write him a note. I don't actually see him very often these days. He's spending most of his nights with Jennifer in her flat in Douglas. She's got him looking at luxury properties all over the island, and she's talking about starting a family right away. I'm certain she's after his money, but he refuses to even consider the idea," Anne told her.

"I hope he doesn't do anything foolish," Bessie said.

"Just being with the girl is foolish," Anne countered. "But I know what you mean. He's promised me that he won't marry her without telling me, but I'm almost afraid to believe him."

"You know Elizabeth is back on the island."

"I do, and I've been trying to find a way to get her and Andy in the same place at the same time. I'm sure they still have feelings for one another, they're both just too stubborn to admit to it."

"You could be right. Maybe I can engineer something. First, though, Andy has to ring me back."

"I'll leave him a note and, if I see him, I'll nag him, as well," Anne promised.

"Thank you," Bessie replied.

With time to fill before dinner, Bessie went up to her office and went back to work on Carree's diaries. By the time Andrew came to collect her, she'd completed two more entries.

"She changed the code again, and it seems as if she's changing it with every entry now," Bessie told him as they made their way to Onchan. "Luckily, she didn't change it much from one entry to the next, and I was able to decipher two more pages."

"So what's going on in Carree's life now?" he asked.

"She's in love again," Bessie replied. "This time with a young man called Stuart Turner. He's only just moved to the island. He's staying with his cousin in Peel and working at the docks. Thus far, I don't think they've actually met, but she's still quite infatuated."

"I hope things go better for her this time."

"I don't expect they will," Bessie told him with a laugh.

The restaurant in Onchan was larger than the one Dan had had in Lonan, but it still wasn't all that large. As Andrew took one of the last parking spaces in the car park,

Bessie began to worry that they'd have a long wait for a table.

"It looks busy," Andrew remarked as they headed for the entrance.

"It should be, assuming the food is as good here as it was in Lonan. It was incredible during the grand opening celebration, anyway."

"Bessie, hello," Carol Jenkins called across the restaurant as they walked inside. "Just give me a minute."

The dining room had around three dozen tables and, from what Bessie could see, there were only a few empty ones. A group of four came in behind Bessie and Andrew while they waited.

Carol greeted Bessie with a hug and then led her and Andrew to a table in a quiet corner. "I hope this is good," she said. "It's lovely that we're busy, but I can try to find you something else if you'd prefer to be closer to the windows." She gestured towards the windows that gave diners a distant sea view.

"This is fine," Bessie told her. "We didn't come for the view."

Carol laughed. "That's good to know. Let me tell you about today's samples, then."

"Yes, please," Bessie said eagerly.

"Well, you know my husband is more than a little crazy in love with Wendy," she said.

Bessie nodded. The couple had struggled with infertility for some time, and Bessie had been delighted when Carol had managed to fall pregnant with their baby girl. "She must be, what, four months old now?" Bessie asked.

"I have pictures," Carol told her with a laugh. "I won't bore you with too many, but I may have to show you one or two before you leave."

"You know I'll be happy to see them all," Bessie assured her.

"Anyway, Wendy isn't allowed food yet. I'm still feeding her myself, which made my husband start to think about milk, which led to cows, which led to today's sampler plate. The main course plate comes with a slice of beef tenderloin, a small serving of beef stroganoff, a scoop of stir-fried beef and vegetables over rice, and a tiny bowl of beef stew."

"Yes, please," Andrew said quickly.

Carol nodded. "The pudding plate is milk-based. A small pot of chocolate mousse, a scoop of caramel ice cream, a square of bread-and-butter pudding, and a handful of homemade milk chocolates."

"Maybe I'll skip dinner and have two puddings," Andrew said.

Bessie shook her head. "You can't do that," she scolded him.

"I would argue, except the dinner plate sounded incredibly good, almost as good as the pudding plate," he laughed.

"You can always have pudding here and take a second serving home with you," Carol suggested with a wink.

Andrew grinned at her. "I may have to do just that," he said.

"Don't forget to bring back some pictures of the baby," Bessie reminded Carol after she'd taken their drink and food order.

"I'll bring them with your drinks," Carol promised before she walked away.

"They seem to be doing a very good business," Andrew said as the door opened and another group of four entered the restaurant.

"Dan's an excellent chef, and Carol works incredibly hard to keep everyone happy. She's good at finding the right staff to help, too. I did wonder if she'd stay home with the baby, but clearly she isn't."

"I am, though," Carol told her with a chuckle as she rejoined them. "I work only one night each week. You just happened to come in on my night this week. I've been coming in to help with lunch a bit more often, but not much. We've worked hard to find great people to help Dan so that I don't have to be here, but I've found that I don't really enjoy being home with the baby all the time, either. Since my mother is living on the island now, too, she's more than happy to look after Wendy whenever I want or need to help out here."

"How nice for all of you," Bessie said.

"Actually, I'm pretty sure my mother wants me to work a good deal more than I do," Carol laughed. "She loves being a grandmother and spending time with Wendy. She's trying to convince me that Dan and I should shut the café for a few days and go away somewhere, just the two of us. I'm not ready to leave Wendy for more than a few hours at a time, though."

Andrew nodded. "They're only little for a very short amount of time. Enjoy it while you can. Once Wendy gets to the terrible twos, you can leave her with your mother for a weekend."

Carol laughed. "That's a great plan."

Andrew and Bessie were talking about a radio programme that they both enjoyed when the food arrived. Bessie took one look at the very full plate she'd been given and sighed.

"I'm not going to have room for pudding," she complained.

"We can box it up for takeaway," Carol assured her. "We do that quite a lot. Dan's been thinking about reducing the number of items on the sample plates to three rather than four, but I think more variety is better."

"Three would probably be more than enough food, but I want every single thing on this plate," Bessie told her.

Carol nodded. "And that's the problem. Dan usually comes up with a list of half a dozen or more possible items for each sampler before he speaks to his suppliers about getting the fresh ingredients. He always struggles to narrow down each sampler to just four items. Maybe he should just try smaller portions of each option."

"That's a better idea," Bessie said.

Half an hour later, her plate was empty and her stomach was full. "Everything was delicious," she said with a happy sigh.

"If Dan ever wants to move to London, he'd be a huge success there," Andrew said as Carol cleared away their plates.

"We aren't planning on ever moving again," Carol replied. "We both love the island and the people we've met here."

"The island is lucky to have you," Bessie said.

"I know you both said you wanted pudding. Would you like me to box it for takeaway?" Carol asked.

Bessie looked at Andrew and shrugged. "I'm full, but the puddings sounded so good that I think I want them right now."

Andrew laughed. "I was thinking the same thing, but I didn't want to sound greedy."

Carol was back with their sweet course a moment later.

"So good," Bessie sighed when she'd cleared the plate. "I think the ice cream was the best part."

"I preferred the chocolate mousse. I could have eaten an entire bowl of that."

"You should sell your ice cream in tubs," Bessie told Carol.

"Dan and I were talking about that the other day, actually," was the reply that surprised Bessie. "Now that we have Wendy, we're both thinking a lot more about the future. Adding a few more income streams would be a very good thing. The restaurant has limited seating, and Dan can prepare only so many meals each day, but we could manufacture fairly large quantities of ice cream that could be sold for weeks or even months." Carol shrugged. "It was just an idea. I'm full of those at the moment."

"I definitely ate too much," Bessie said as they walked out of the building after Andrew had paid the bill.

"It was worth every single calorie," Andrew replied, patting his stomach.

"And the skies have cleared. It's a lovely evening," Bessie said, thinking that maybe she'd have a walk on the beach when they got back to Laxey. She'd walked on the beach at all hours for years, but after her cottage had been broken into during a murder investigation over a year earlier, she'd become more reluctant to leave the cottage unattended after dark.

"It's the perfect night for a walk," Andrew said as he parked outside of Bessie's cottage.

"You're right. Shall we?"

The pair strolled hand in hand down the beach in a silence broken only by the sound of the waves slapping gently against the sand. They walked as far as Thie yn Traie and then turned back towards Bessie's cottage.

"I can't help but feel as if we're closing in on a solution in our case," Andrew said at the door to Treoghe Bwaane. "It may be misplaced optimism, of course."

"I feel the same way. Let's hope you hear back from Pennsylvania soon," Bessie replied.

They agreed to meet for breakfast for a change, and then Bessie went into her cottage and went to bed.

CHAPTER 14

"Good morning," Andrew said when Bessie opened the door to his knock the next morning. "Ready for breakfast?"

"I'm starving," Bessie replied. "I took a long walk and then curled up a with book to keep myself from eating something, and now I'm ready to eat just about anything."

"I thought we could go into Ramsey and find somewhere there."

"There's a small café on the high street that does American-style breakfasts. Waffles and pancakes with maple syrup and lots and lots of bacon."

"I'm sold," Andrew laughed.

Bessie put on her shoes and reached for her handbag. The phone stopped her on her way to the door.

"I should let the machine get it," she muttered as she reached for the receiver.

"Hello?"

"Miss Cubbon? This is Erica Tucker, just ringing you back."

"Oh, hello," Bessie said, trying not to sound as surprised as she was feeling.

"I understand you're interested in buying a property in Liverpool and wanted to discuss financing," Erica continued.

"Yes, er, I mean, I did, um…" Bessie stopped and took a deep breath. "I'm sorry, but I'm not actually interested in any such thing. I was ringing only because I was trying to find you."

"To find me? I don't understand."

"Grace was worried about you."

"Grace? Grace Christian? Except she's Grace Watterson now. I keep forgetting. Why was Grace worried about me?"

"She texted you a few times and you didn't reply," Bessie explained. The explanation sounded somewhat foolish as she said it.

"Oh, dear," Erica exclaimed. "I forgot to let her know about my new number."

"You have a new mobile number?"

"My mobile was stolen, or rather, it was lost and then stolen, or so I believe. One day I had it, and then the next day I couldn't find it anywhere. I must have dropped it somewhere, but I don't know where. Anyway, I had to get a new phone and a new number, and it's been awful trying to let everyone know."

"I can't imagine."

"I don't have anyone's numbers, of course. They were all in my phone. Do you have Grace's number, by any chance? I'll text her right away and let her know that I'm perfectly fine and just a terrible friend."

Bessie laughed. "She'll be very relieved to hear from you," she said before she gave the woman Grace's number.

"I never meant to worry anyone. And of course, I've been away from work for a few days, having a short holiday with a friend, so she couldn't even reach me here or at home. I'm surprised she didn't ring the police."

"She was going to ring them today, although I suspect she would have simply spoken to Hugh."

Erica laughed. "Of course. No doubt he knows all about it, even if she hasn't yet filed a missing person report. Was she really going to report me missing today?"

"That was the plan. She didn't want to be too hasty, in case you were simply having a holiday or something, but she was genuinely concerned."

"I'm actually deeply touched," Erica said. "Living here in a big city, on my own, I sometimes feel as if I'm alone in the world. It's nice to know that Grace is looking out for me, anyway."

"Well, that's one mystery solved," Bessie told Andrew when she put the phone down. "Erica Tucker is alive and well and simply has a new mobile phone."

"I'm really glad to hear that," Andrew replied. "I was going to ring my friend later today."

Feeling as if a weight had been lifted off of her shoulders, Bessie followed Andrew out to his car. They were in Ramsey a short while later. The café was somewhat busy, but they didn't have to wait long for a table.

"Pancakes and bacon," Andrew decided.

"Waffles," Bessie said. "I can make pancakes at home, but not waffles."

"We do have waffle machines for sale, if you're interested," the waitress told her.

"No, thank you," Bessie replied firmly. "If I had a machine, I'd feel as if I had to use it, and then I'd eat waffles far too frequently. They're delicious, but they aren't exactly nutritious."

"Did you want chocolate chips in your waffles?" the waitress asked.

Bessie shook her head. "I'm tempted, but I think I'd rather have them plain with lots of butter and syrup."

"That's how I prefer them, too," the waitress told her.

After breakfast, Andrew and Bessie wandered through the shops. Andrew bought a few gifts for members of his family, and Bessie picked out a few secondhand books from the various charity shops.

"I was going to suggest that we get lunch somewhere, but I'm still feeling rather full," Andrew said after they'd walked the length of the high street and back again.

"Me too," Bessie admitted. "I think I may skip lunch altogether."

Andrew's phone buzzed before he could reply. He read a text message and then sighed. "I'm going to need to go back to the cottages," he said apologetically. "I need to ring my daughter, and it could take a while."

"That's fine," Bessie replied. She was more than happy to go home and spend some time with Carree, or maybe a good book.

Bessie was lost in the adventures of a widow who'd been left with a very special little black book full of contacts when her phone rang a few hours later.

"I know I'm right next door, but I'm waiting for someone to ring me back," Andrew said when she answered. "I've heard back from Pennsylvania, and we have some things to discuss. Do you want to see if John, Doona, and Hugh are available for an impromptu meeting tonight?"

"I'll see what I can arrange."

"We can meet in your cottage or mine, maybe around six? If someone can bring takeaway with them, I'll pay them back," he added. "Tell them to bring pudding, as well."

He ended the conversation before Bessie could reply. "I could make a pudding," she muttered as she put the phone down. It took her a minute to look through her recipes and her cupboards.

"Doona? It's Bessie. Andrew wants to have a meeting tonight at my cottage. I don't know if you and John are available or not."

"I think we can manage it," Doona replied. "What time?"

"Six."

"I'll ring you back if that's a problem. Otherwise, we'll be there."

"Can you bring dinner, too?" Bessie asked.

Doona laughed. "Of course."

After a moment of indecision, Bessie rang Grace.

"I wasn't certain when Hugh was working today," she told her. "And I wanted to be sure that you've heard from Erica."

"I have. Thank you so much. She laughed at me, but then she told me that she really appreciated that I was worried. I think she feels a bit alone, especially since her mother doesn't really remember her anymore."

"She seemed a lovely young woman. I'm glad she's safe."

"Me too, but you wanted Hugh?"

"Andrew has an update for us, and he was hoping we could all meet in my cottage around six tonight," Bessie explained.

"You're in luck, actually, as Hugh was meant to have class, but his professor just cancelled it because he's unwell."

"I hope you weren't planning on a nice evening together because of the unexpected cancellation."

Grace laughed. "We might have been, but I already had plans for tonight. I've been trying to get together with my friends on nights when Hugh has classes. Tonight my friend Alice and I are taking our babies to the pool complex in Douglas. They have a special mother and baby session one evening a week in the quiet pool."

"How nice."

"It's fun, but it definitely isn't quiet."

With that job out of the way, Bessie went back to her book. Everything was neatly wrapped up by the last page, and Bessie sighed as she put her book back on the shelf. "If only problems in real life could be worked out in a set number of pages," she muttered to herself.

Hugh was the first to arrive, just before six.

"What's happened?" he asked Bessie after he'd hugged her tightly.

"I wish I knew. Andrew just said that he'd heard back from the detective in Pennsylvania. He didn't tell me anything else."

"Well, that's frustrating," Hugh laughed.

"I made chocolate chip cookies," Bessie told him.

"I don't suppose you'll let me have one now."

"No, I won't," Bessie agreed.

"I can wait," Hugh said, looking as if waiting was the last thing he wanted to do.

John and Doona arrived a moment later, carrying several large boxes.

"We got Chinese," Doona announced. "It came from a place in Ramsey. I hope it's all still hot."

By the time she and Bessie had all of the small boxes of food arranged across the counter, Andrew was at the door.

"Something smells good," he said.

They were all filling plates when someone knocked.

"Who could that be?" Bessie asked as she headed for the door.

"Ah, yes, I did mention our little gathering to Charles and Harry," Andrew said quickly. "I may have inadvertently invited them to join us."

"Inadvertently?" Bessie echoed. She shook her head and then opened the door.

"Good evening," Harry said.

"Good evening," Bessie replied.

Charles muttered something that Bessie didn't even try to understand. Instead, she took a step backwards. "Do come in," she invited them. "We'll need more chairs. I hope we'll all fit."

John and Hugh carried in chairs from the dining room and squeezed them in around the small kitchen table. It fit four people comfortably, but there seemed no way that seven people would be able to eat dinner together around it.

"Help yourself to something to eat," Bessie said to the new arrivals, choosing to ignore the tight squeeze at the table.

A short while later, everyone was squashed together with their plates and drinks. Although it annoyed Bessie that Harry hadn't taken anything to eat, she had to admit to herself that he'd have had nowhere to put his plate if he'd filled one. As it was, Hugh was trying to eat from a plate that was near the centre of the table because the space in front of him was taken up by Doona's and Andrew's plates.

"This is cosy," Andrew said. When his eyes met Bessie's they both began to laugh. After a moment, everyone at the table joined in.

"This better be important," Charles said after the laughter stopped. "I mean, we were going to meet tomorrow anyway. The only thing I can imagine us needing an emergency meeting for would be a confession."

"Sadly, we don't have a confession," Andrew told him. "But we do seem to have started asking the right questions."

"What does that mean?" Bessie asked.

"It means Harvey has given the police some interesting answers to the questions that we sent," he replied.

"Stop teasing and just tell us what you've found out," Harry said tightly.

Andrew took a bite of his meal and then a sip of his drink. "Sorry, let me start at the beginning. The detective in Pennsylvania rang Harvey and asked him if they could have another chat about the case. He reckoned that Harvey was more than happy to agree. They made an appointment for the next day, and the detective asked Harvey to bring with him a rough timeline for the weekend when he came to the station."

"That was clever," Bessie murmured as Andrew stopped for another bite.

"It also seems to have worried Harvey. When he turned up for the meeting, he brought a lawyer with him," Andrew told them.

"His father?" Doona asked.

"No, a criminal defense attorney," Andrew replied.

"That seems to be almost an admission of guilt," Bessie suggested.

"He said it was for his protection, that he was concerned what the others might be saying about what happened that weekend," Andrew told her.

"What the others might be saying?" Bessie repeated. "All because he was asked for a timeline?"

"We don't know that for certain, but the police in Pennsylvania certainly think so. I've made copies of the timeline that Harvey gave them when he spoke to them. Let's take a look at that now."

He passed around sheets of paper. Bessie slid back from the table so that she could look over her copy.

"It's very vague," she said.

"He reminded the police that he'd been drinking heavily and had no reason to be paying attention to the time," Andrew told her.

"According to this, he was passed out in bed the night of the murder," Doona said. "I don't remember him claiming before to have been passed out that night."

"If he truly was passed out, Mary Ellen doesn't have an alibi," Harry remarked.

"Not that we were taking the word of a very drunk man as an alibi," Bessie added.

Harry nodded. "Of course not, but it's interesting that he's seemingly no longer concerned with providing her with an alibi."

"Indeed," Andrew said. "He was asked about the current state of his relationship with the people who were at the cabin that weekend. He told the police that he hasn't spoken to any of them in years."

"Really?" Bessie asked. "Don't any of them come back to Greenview for the holidays or anything?"

"When they attempted to pin him down, Harvey admitted to having seen Mike about a year ago around Christmas. Greenview is a small town, after all. Apparently, Mike was there visiting some family, and they crossed paths at a local restaurant. Harvey had similar stories about seeing all of the others in the past few years, all except for Mary Ellen."

"Because she hasn't been back to Greenview," Bessie guessed.

"At least not as far as Harvey knows," Andrew replied. "He hasn't seen her, and he hasn't heard anyone saying that she'd been in town, either. Considering they were a couple for so many years, I have to believe that someone would have told him if she'd come back to town," Andrew said.

"So, regardless of chance meetings, Harvey hasn't stayed in touch with any of them," Doona said.

"Surprising, considering they all still have family there," Charles remarked.

"Julie's death must have been traumatic for all of them," Doona said. "Maybe they all wanted to forget it ever happened."

"What else did Harvey have to say?" Bessie asked.

As she was speaking, Doona stood up. "I'll just clear the dishes," she said.

"Does anyone want tea?" Bessie asked.

She switched on the kettle and then started a pot of coffee as well. It took her only a moment to fill a plate with the chocolate chip cookies she'd baked earlier in the day.

"Did you make these because you didn't have chocolate chips in your waffles?" Andrew asked as Bessie put the plate on the table.

She laughed. "Now that you mention it, I probably did, but without realising it. I just felt in the mood for something with chocolate chips. It was probably our breakfast that put the idea in my head, though."

Once everyone was back at the table with drinks and cookies, Bessie repeated her question. "What else did Harvey have to say?"

"The last thing that he was asked about was the fight with Mary Ellen," Andrew replied. "My colleague in Pennsylvania said that Harvey seemed shocked by the question and that he didn't seem to know how to reply."

"Which suggests he was busy coming up with a lie," Harry suggested.

"Possibly," Andrew said. "What he eventually told the police was that the fight had taken place far too long ago for him to remember what it had been about. He said something about silly teenaged bickering and told them that the entire thing had been completely inconsequential."

"A lie, in other words," Bessie said firmly.

"The detective then asked him how long he'd been involved with Julie during those months when he and Mary Ellen had been apart. He said that Harvey looked even more shocked and then tried to insist that he'd never gone out with Julie," Andrew said.

"I'm more inclined to believe Robbie on that point," Bessie said.

"So are the police," Andrew told her. "After Harvey got done talking, the detective gave him a lecture about lying to the police and withholding evidence in a murder investigation. He told me that Harvey looked quite shaken by the time he'd reminded him that Julie had been brutally murdered and that she deserved justice."

"He's a lawyer, which means he's a good actor," Charles suggested.

"In the end, Harvey agreed to spend some time trying to remember everything that he can about the months leading up to the murder. He said he'd dig out his old yearbook and his photo albums and see what he can find that might trigger his memory. For what it's worth, my colleague in Pennsylvania actually believes that Harvey is going to do what he can to help. We'll see."

"Is that it?" Charles asked. "I mean, I know it's progress, but I was expecting a confession, or at least a solid lead."

"Harvey did say one other thing that may be of interest," Andrew told him. "He suggested to the police that they really ought to question Mary Ellen more closely. He said that he was pretty sure she'd remember what they'd fought about in the months before the murder. He also reckoned that she'd be able to draw up a timeline for the entire weekend, because she was the only one not actually drinking."

"Not drinking or not drinking much?" Bessie asked. "She said in her statement that she drank less than the others, but that she was still drinking for much of the weekend."

"According to Harvey, she barely drank anything alcoholic during the weekend, although he didn't really pay attention to it at the time. It was only later, when he thought back, that he remembered that she was uncharacteristically sober for much of the weekend."

"'Uncharacteristically sober,'" Bessie repeated. "So she usually drank a lot?"

"Actually, according to Harvey's most recent statement, she didn't always drink much. When she and Harvey went out, she often drove, and then she wouldn't drink much because she didn't want a drink driving arrest on her record, not when she was heading to law school."

"I wonder if she drinks and drives now," John said.

"She's never been stopped for drink driving," Andrew told him. "She lives in a village that's owned by the ski resort where she works. I was told that she skis everywhere she needs to go."

"I hope she isn't skiing drunk," Hugh said.

"I can't wait to see what she has to say when the police talk to her again," Doona said. "I don't know that I think that she killed Julie, but I definitely think she's hiding something."

Andrew nodded. "We'll meet tomorrow afternoon as planned. I hope to have more information for you by that time."

CHAPTER 15

Doona did the washing-up as Harry and Charles spoke briefly with Andrew and then left. Hugh wasn't far behind, leaving with a small bag of cookies in his hand. John and Doona left with Andrew once the chairs had been moved back to the dining room and the kitchen was tidy. It was raining again, so Bessie gave up on the idea of taking another walk and found another book to enjoy instead. She was yawning over it a few hours later, so she took herself off to bed.

THE RAIN HAD STOPPED by the time Bessie went out for her walk the next morning. She walked past Thie yn Traie, nearly as far as the new houses, before she turned back towards home. It wasn't until she was nearly back at Treoghe Bwaane that she spotted the person sitting on the large rock behind her cottage. Her heart skipped a beat before she could assure herself that it was probably Pat. He often sat there to think. Bessie had found him there at all hours of the day and night. As she got closer to home, however, she realised it wasn't Pat at all.

"Andy? What brings you here?" she asked in a low voice, touching the man on the shoulder.

He started and then sighed. "I was hoping to get away without you noticing me," he said as he moved over so that she could sit next to him on the rock.

"I can simply go inside," she offered, even though she had no intention of letting the man get away without hearing a few things from her.

"No, don't do that," he countered. "Mum said you rang. I've been meaning to ring you back, but I've been really busy."

"I rang because Jasper was quite upset to find some of his menu items on your catering menu," Bessie replied.

Andy sighed. "Jennifer and I were talking about ideas for her catering menu. She was playing around with the layout design while we were talking, so she plugged some of the ideas we were discussing into the draft. When she went to print out the actual menu to give to the printer, she accidentally printed the wrong one. Unfortunately, she didn't notice until she'd had a thousand copies printed and she'd started giving them out."

Bessie raised an eyebrow. "That's a pretty serious mistake to make."

"She's apologised to Jasper and given everyone the correct menu now," Andy said with a shrug. "Everyone makes mistakes."

"Indeed, but this is her business. She should be proofreading and double-checking everything. She could have done serious damage to her reputation and to yours."

"But she didn't. It's all sorted now."

"Good. So what brings you down here today?"

"I like to come down here and watch the sea. This was my

refuge when I was a teenager, and sometimes it still feels as if it's the only safe place in the world."

"Why do you need a safe place?"

"I don't need a safe place, exactly. Things are just really busy. I'm still trying to find the right location for my restaurant. Jennifer has her party planning business. That takes up a great deal of her time at all hours of the day and night. She's trying to get a catering business established as well, in case the party planning business struggles against the new competition."

"A catering business where you'll do the catering?" Bessie asked.

"Of course, in the beginning, anyway. I'm doing my best to teach Jennifer how to make everything on the menu so that she won't need my help forever, but for now, well, she's still learning."

"But you are going to open your own restaurant one day."

"One day, yes. That's always been my dream. But helping Jennifer is important to me, too. She's the woman I'm going to marry, after all."

"Have you set a date yet?"

"Jennifer wants to just run away somewhere and get married without any fuss, but I don't plan on doing this ever again, and I want you and my mother to be there."

"I'm flattered."

Andy shrugged. "I'll always be grateful to you for everything that you did for me."

"You can repay me by getting your restaurant open," Bessie told him. "I want to see you fulfill your dream."

"I'm working on it, in my spare time."

"Have you found a house to buy?"

"I've been staying in Jennifer's flat most nights. She thinks we should buy something in one of the new developments right on the promenade."

Bessie made a face. "I've never been interested in living in a flat. I did it once, for a few weeks, and I was miserable. There were always people coming and going next door and below me. I much prefer my little cottage by the sea."

"And if I could find a little cottage by the sea, I think I'd buy it. There simply aren't that many places right on the water and, at the moment, none of them are for sale."

"But if you buy a flat in Douglas, you won't have the money to buy your dream house when it does become available."

"I have quite a lot of money," Andy laughed. "But you're right. I don't want to buy a flat in Douglas and then keep looking at other properties. I suppose I need to decide whether I can live in a flat in Douglas or not."

"It would be convenient if you end up having your restaurant there."

"I don't know that I want to have the restaurant in Douglas. There's a lot of competition there. I was considering Onchan, but Dan and Carol Jenkins have just opened there, and I can't compete with Dan and his amazing sampler plates."

"You wouldn't be competing with him, though, not really. He does what he does very well, but you'd be an altogether different sort of restaurant."

Andy shrugged. "I'm not sure what sort of restaurant I want, though. I thought I was going to go all out and have a high-end place, but the more I think about it, the more I think I want to make simple, straightforward food with the freshest possible ingredients. The puddings, well, they'll be complicated and fancy, though."

Bessie laughed. "I'll eat there at least once a week," she promised.

Andy grinned at her. "I'm counting on that."

For a moment, they both sat and watched the wave. Andy sighed before he spoke again.

"How's Elizabeth?" he asked in a low voice.

"It's been a long six months for her," Bessie replied.

"I find that hard to believe. She was on holiday," he said bitterly.

Bessie opened her mouth and then snapped it shut. It wasn't her place to tell him about Mary's illness.

"I assume she's planning to restart her party planning business," Andy said after a pause.

"I believe so, yes."

"I hope the island is big enough to support two such businesses. Both Jennifer and I want to see her succeed, as long as Jennifer can continue to do well, too."

"I'm glad to hear that." Bessie hesitated and then spoke again. "I thought you and Elizabeth were good together."

Andy made a noise. "Sometimes, maybe," he said. "It was complicated."

Bessie nodded. "I just hope you'll take things slowly with Jennifer. You haven't known her for very long."

"Did my mother tell you that she's just after my money?"

"Is she just after your money?"

Andy laughed. "Obviously, I don't think so. It's weird, having money, after a lifetime of being poor. I'm probably not as suspicious of people and their motives as I should be, but I didn't tell Jennifer about the money until we'd already been seeing one another for a few weeks. She seemed to like me well enough when I was just some guy who'd just come back from catering college."

Bessie chose her words very carefully. "I think it's possible that she already knew who you were before she met you," she said softly.

There was a long pause before Andy suddenly jumped off the rock. "No one believes that she might actually care about me for me," he said angrily. "Am I such a terrible person that it's only my money that makes me attractive?"

"Of course not," Bessie told him. "You're a wonderful person, and Jennifer is lucky to have found you. I just want to be certain that she knows that."

"We're lucky to have found each other, and we're very happy together," he said. "Maybe she's right. Maybe we should just run away together."

Bessie frowned. "I'm sorry if I upset you, but I hope you appreciate that I'm concerned because I care about you. I will be very hurt if I don't get invited to the wedding."

She watched as a dozen different emotions flashed over the man's face. Eventually, he sighed. "I need to go."

"Bring Jennifer for dinner again soon," Bessie invited. "I'd like another opportunity to get to know her."

"I'll ring you," he promised before he turned and walked up the beach towards the parking area next to Bessie's cottage.

She watched him go and then sighed as she slid off the rock. That he'd been there at all suggested that life with Jennifer wasn't all that rosy. He'd never sought refuge behind Treoghe Bwaane when he'd been involved with Elizabeth, at least not as far as she knew.

Andrew collected Bessie just before midday, and they went and had lunch in Ramsey before the meeting. Bessie was distracted, her mind on Andy, so she barely noticed that Andrew was just as unfocussed on making conversation with her over their meal. It wasn't until they were walking into the conference room on the top floor of the Seaview that Bessie dragged her thoughts back to the case at hand.

"Have you heard back from whoever was going to interview Mary Ellen?" she asked Andrew as they both filled plates with biscuits and scones.

"I have, but let's wait until everyone is here to discuss what she said," he replied.

Bessie nodded. "I'm a bit distracted today," she said as an apology.

"I did wonder why you didn't ask me that as soon as you saw me," Andrew replied.

"I would have done, if I hadn't been thinking about other things," Bessie replied. "Never mind. I'm focussed on the case now."

The others trickled in while Bessie nibbled her way through a biscuit and drank a cup of tea. As Harry took his seat, Bessie quickly got up and refilled her drink. Andrew was ready to start when she sat back down.

"Again, I have copies of Mary Ellen's interview," Andrew began. "I'm going to go over it with you, though. The detective who spoke with her, his name is Clint Boxer, is hoping for some suggestions on the best way to approach the next round of questioning."

"She said something interesting, then," Harry guessed.

"She said quite a few interesting things," Andrew replied. "Clint asked her the same questions that were asked of Harvey, and she gave similarly vague replies. Clint asked her to write up a timeline, and she gave him a very sketchy outline of the weekend's events. He was about to let her go when he happened to comment that, as he understood it, Harvey had been more forthcoming."

"And that set her off," Harry suggested.

"It did indeed. Clint said it felt as if she'd just been waiting to hear that information. He said she went very still and then began to cry. You can read her exact words in the statement, but basically she claimed that Harvey was abusive and that she'd been hiding that from everyone for over twenty years."

"I don't believe it," Harry said flatly.

Bessie wasn't sure what to believe. "She went out with him for all those years, even while he was abusing her?" she asked.

"She told Clint that she'd felt forced to stay with him because both of their families expected it. Her mother had been planning for her to marry Harvey since the day she'd been born," Andrew told her.

"Surely her mother wouldn't have wanted her to stay with a man who was abusive," Bessie argued.

"According to Mary Ellen, it was mostly verbal and emotional abuse, which is difficult to prove. He rarely got physical, and usually took care not to leave any marks on her," Andrew replied.

"Is that the reason she gave for why they broke up, then?" John asked.

"It was. She said they'd had a particularly bad fight and he'd hurt her quite badly. She'd ended things and promised herself that she'd never get back together with him."

"But she did get back together with him," Bessie said with a sigh.

"According to Mary Ellen, that was because of pressure from her mother and from her friends. It was the end of senior year. There was prom and graduation and a great many parties. She didn't want to do all of that alone, especially not while Harvey was seeing a succession of other women. She agreed to get back together, but under her terms."

"Which were what?" Doona demanded.

"She had photographs of what he'd done to her during that last big fight. She threatened to send them to his fancy Ivy League school if he ever touched her again. They were together for parties and events, but privately, they were barely speaking, or so she claims. That's why Harvey spent most of the weekend watching television by himself while the others played games and had fun together."

"She had photographs?" Harry asked.

"Not only had them, but had them with her," Andrew replied.

Harry frowned. "Had them with her in Colorado yesterday? As in she carries them around in her handbag?"

"She'd grabbed them when she knew she was going to be questioned about the murder," Andrew told him. "She claimed that she and Harvey had an agreement. She wouldn't tell anyone about the abuse as long as he stayed well away from her."

"So why break the agreement?" Hugh wondered.

"She seemed to think that Harvey may have said something to implicate her in Julie's murder," Andrew explained. "According to Mary Ellen, as soon as she'd heard that Julie had been killed, she'd known that Harvey had done it. She was too afraid of him to say anything, though, and she's been keeping quiet ever since."

"I don't believe it," Harry said. "What did the photos show?"

"Clint emailed me scans of a few of them, but it's very hard to see anything in them. He said they aren't much better in person. Basically, they show bruises on an arm and a leg, but there's nothing in them to tie them to any person, place, or date."

"She's making it all up because she killed Julie," Harry said flatly.

"That's one possibility," Andrew said. "One that Clint is leaning towards, actually. He found the entire exchange with Mary Ellen rather odd. He said he felt as if she was reading all of her replies from a script, but that she kept losing her place or something."

"She's been anticipating the questions for years," Harry

suggested. "She's been expecting to be accused of murder and she's ready to try to frame Harvey for the crime."

"Did she say anything about motive?" Bessie asked.

"She said that Harvey had gone out with Julie a few times when she and Harvey had been apart, and that once Julie and Mike had their fight, he'd decided that he'd go down and have sex with Julie since Mary Ellen obviously wasn't going to let him touch her. Mary Ellen reckons that Julie said no, so Harvey killed her," Andrew replied.

"Let me guess, she's prepared to testify that Harvey left the room in the middle of the night," Harry said.

Andrew nodded. "Clint doesn't believe much, if any, of her story, but he isn't certain where to go next with his questioning. For now, he's told her that he's going to request that Harvey be taken in for additional questioning. He's going to have Mary Ellen picked up and brought in just after midday, Colorado time."

"She'll have another story ready if it becomes clear that Clint isn't buying the first one," Harry said. "I wonder what Harvey is going to say, though."

"They're five hours behind us in Pennsylvania, so it's only around ten o'clock there," Andrew said. "I should have an email from the detective there later today, though."

"Harvey is going to have his own version of events, and it's going to be very different from Mary Ellen's," Harry said. "He's going to deny the abuse and suggest that Mary Ellen killed Julie."

"Someone should talk to his ex-wives," Doona said. "If he was abusive to Mary Ellen, he was probably abusive to them as well."

Andrew nodded and made a note. "Any thoughts on what Clint can ask Mary Ellen?"

"Aside from asking about whatever Harvey says, maybe he can try again on the timeline," John suggested. "Now that she's telling all, maybe she'll be willing to do a proper timeline."

"Except it will all be lies," Harry said. "She'll probably go out of her way to find places where she can put Harvey and Julie alone together."

"Why would she let Harvey get away with murder for all these years? Didn't she have any feelings for Julie?" Bessie asked. "They were supposed to be friends, weren't they? Surely Julie deserved better."

"That's very clever," Harry said. "That might trigger all sorts of interesting revelations."

They talked for a while longer, but didn't come up with anything else. An hour later, Bessie found herself pacing around her kitchen, desperately wondering what was happening in Pennsylvania. "At least all of this is keeping me from worrying about Andy," she muttered to herself as she waited for Andrew to come over and tell her what he'd learned in his latest emails.

"Things are getting interesting now," he told Bessie when he came to collect her for dinner some hours later. "Harvey was furious when he was told that Mary Ellen had accused him of being abusive. He said that she'd been threatening for the last fifteen years to tell the police that he'd hit her when they'd been together, and that he wasn't going to let her dictate how he lived his life anymore. He insisted on giving the police a new statement about the weekend at the cabin, and he basically accused Mary Ellen of murder."

"She isn't going to be very happy about that."

"It will probably be tomorrow before I hear back from Clint," Andrew sighed. "I shouldn't be telling you anything, really, not until I can tell the whole unit what's happening."

∽

He got a chance to tell them everything a few days later. Bessie had already heard the entire story, but she promised to pretend to be shocked as Andrew told the others.

"Mary Ellen has been arrested for murdering Julie Carter," he announced as soon as everyone was sitting around the conference room table in the penthouse room. "When the police told Harvey about Mary Ellen's accusations, he made several accusations of his own. Then Clint spoke to Mary Ellen."

"She was at the top of my list the entire time," Harry muttered.

Bessie frowned. "But not mine."

"What did she have to say?" Doona demanded.

"Clint told her what Harvey had said, and she insisted it was all lies, made up to hide the fact that he was an abuser. Then Clint asked her what Bessie had said about lying to protect Harvey instead of doing what was right for her friend Julie. Apparently, Mary Ellen just stared at him for a minute and then told him flat out that she and Julie were not ever friends."

"Oh, dear," Doona exclaimed.

"When Clint asked her what she meant, Mary Ellen let loose a string of obscenities about Julie, calling her the woman that had ruined everything."

"Ruined everything?" Bessie echoed.

"She claimed that she and Harvey were happy and crazy about one another until he got it in his head that he wanted to sleep with Julie. From what Mary Ellen said, prior to that he used to sleep with other women on occasion, but they had an agreement about it. Basically, as long as it was just physical, she didn't mind."

"How awful," Doona blurted out.

"Apparently, Julie was the first woman who said no. She insisted that she wouldn't sleep with him while he was involved with Mary Ellen, so he broke up with Mary Ellen so that he could sleep with Julie," Andrew told them.

"Mary Ellen was better off without him," Bessie said.

"I agree, but she didn't. It wasn't just her mother who had plans for the pair to marry one day. Mary Ellen was furious with Julie and with Harvey. She also said that Julie's death had simply made things worse, because Harvey seemed to think that she'd killed Julie. After she'd told Clint all of this, she seemed to realise what she was saying and began to backtrack, claiming that she'd been grateful to Julie for coming between her and her abuser, but the damage had been done. The more he questioned her, the more convoluted her story became until Mary Ellen actually confessed to killing Julie, although she's claiming it was self-defense."

"The girl was asleep when she was stabbed," Harry said dryly.

"Yes, I don't think the courts are going to believe it was self-defense," Andrew agreed. "Anyway, we have a confession of sorts. We've solved another case."

"And I was right about the killer from the start," Harry said happily.

Bessie sat back with a frown on her face. "I was quite wrong," she said in a low voice.

"And none of that matters. You both contributed to the solution, as did all the other members of the team. I'm really proud of all of you. We're three for three, which is amazing. I'm going to have to look for something more challenging for next time."

"I think that was quite hard enough," Harry replied. "It took us a while to get to grips with it all."

"But we got there in the end. Whatever the result of the trial, we found Julie's killer," Andrew said. "We should celebrate over dinner tonight."

Everyone agreed, even Bessie, who wasn't really feeling in

the mood for a celebration. The case had left her feeling sad and out of sorts. A young girl had died at the hands of someone who was meant to be her friend. Whatever the motive, it was terribly sad.

A WEEK LATER, Andrew was ready to head back to London.

"I'll see you in the new year," he told Bessie after they'd had breakfast together in Treoghe Bwaane. "I hope you have a wonderful Christmas."

Bessie nodded. Things were going to be busy for the next fortnight leading up to Christmas. She had Christmas at the Castle to get through; presents to buy, wrap, and distribute; and a great deal of food to prepare and enjoy with friends. As soon as her celebrations were over, she was going to be heading to Derbyshire for a wedding, as well.

"I hope you have a happy Christmas," she told him. "Enjoy your time with your family, and I'll see you in mid-January."

Andrew honked as he drove away, leaving Bessie waving on her doorstep. She pushed her door shut and walked to the sink to start washing up the breakfast dishes. After three cases, she still wasn't entirely certain how she felt about the cold case unit. It was emotionally difficult work, but it was also incredibly satisfying when they got results.

When the dishes were washed, dried, and put away, Bessie went into the sitting room and picked out one of her favourite murder mysteries. *Fictional murders are much more satisfying than real ones*, she thought as she opened the book to the first page.

THE DURAND FILE

AN AUNT BESSIE COLD CASE MYSTERY

Release date: October 15, 2021
Turn the page for a sneak peek.

With all the time he's spending on the island running his cold case unit, Andrew Cheatham is considering buying a house there. Bessie is happy to go along on the hunt with him, but they're both surprised and upset to discover a fire raging at one of the houses he's considering purchasing. It's even more upsetting to learn that the fire was started deliberately.

Meanwhile, the cold case unit has not one, but two murders to consider. The two men died two years apart, but the French police are convinced that the cases are connected. While Bessie is happy to agree that the cases are connected, she's not convinced that the same person was responsible for both deaths.

Can Bessie and the cold case unit work out what really happened to the two men? Bessie also wants to help the police discover who set the fire at Christian Christian's house, but does she have time to do that, as well? And will she ever have a chance to really get to know the two police inspectors she's working with on the unit who never seem to have time to socialise with Bessie and her friends?

A SNEAK PEEK AT THE DURAND FILE
AN AUNT BESSIE COLD CASE MYSTERY

Release date: October 15, 2021

Please excuse any typos or minor errors. I have not yet completed final edits on this title.

Chapter One

"I told the estate agent that we'd be there around one o'clock," Andrew Cheatham said to Elizabeth Cubbon as she handed him a plate of food.

Elizabeth, known as Bessie to nearly everyone, glanced at the clock. "We've time for a leisurely lunch, then," she said happily before joining him at her kitchen table with her own full plate.

"I would have been more than happy to buy you lunch somewhere," Andrew told her before he took his first bite.

"I know, but we seem to go out for a great many meals while you're here. I thought it would be nice for you to have something homemade for a change," Bessie countered.

Andrew nodded. "This is delicious. I tend to have most of

A SNEAK PEEK AT THE DURAND FILE

my meals in restaurants when I'm at home in London, as well. This is a real treat."

"It's only a roast chicken and a few vegetables. It wasn't any bother."

"Well, it's delicious and I'm greatly appreciative."

The pair ate in a companionable silence for a few minutes in Bessie's cosy kitchen. She'd owned her small cottage on Laxey Beach for more years than she wanted to acknowledge. While most people would have suggested that the kitchen needed updating, everything still worked and Bessie was more than happy to leave it exactly as it was. It would be up to her relatives in America to decide what to do with the cottage after she was gone. She'd already extended it twice, but she had no plans to do anything further to it in the future.

"I hope you don't mind doing a bit of house hunting with me," Andrew said after a while.

"Not at all. I enjoy going around other people's houses. I'm always fascinated by how other people live."

Andrew chuckled. "I hadn't really thought of house hunting in that way, but you're right, of course. You do get to see how other people live. I may have seen rather too much of that when I was working, of course."

Bessie nodded. Andrew has been a police inspector with Scotland Yard for many years. "I was surprised when you said you were looking at houses," Bessie replied.

"As I'm spending around a fortnight here every month, it simply makes sense to consider buying a house here. That isn't to say that I'm not comfortable in my holiday cottage next door, just that I think I might be more comfortable in a home of my own."

There was a row of holiday cottages that stretched just past Bessie's cottage along the beach. The last cottage was just a few feet away from the stairs that led to Thie yn Traie, a huge mansion that was perched on the cliffs above the sea. The holiday cottages were owned by Bessie's friends, Thomas and Maggie Shimmin. They didn't usually hire them out in the winter months, but they'd made an exception for Andrew, letting him rent the cottage closest to Bessie's each month during his visits.

"So you're planning on coming across for some time to come," Bessie replied.

Andrew nodded. "The cold case unit has already been much more successful than we anticipated it would be when we started out. It's attracting a great deal of attention in certain circles and I've been flooded with requests for help from around world. We could start considering two or three cases each month for the next ten years and still not get through them all."

"But we're still going to only look at a single case each month?"

"For the time being, anyway. We're still really just getting started. No one expected us to solve our first three cases, least of all me. If I'd known how things were going to go, I might have looked into buying a house before the first meeting."

"Surely, Scotland Yard is paying for your rental cottage, though. Are they going to buy your house for you?"

Andrew shook his head. "That would be nice, but, no, they aren't. They are paying for the cottage rental, in the same way that they're paying for the Seaview for Charles and Harry, but if I buy the house, they'll switch to paying me a small housing allowance instead."

Charles Morris and Harry Blake were two of the other members of the cold case unit that Andrew had set up some months earlier. Bessie and three of her island-based friends made up the rest of the unit. They met for several days each month to discuss a cold case and make suggestions for new avenues that the police might explore. Charles, Harry, and Andrew flew over from London each month for the meetings, as that was more cost effective than flying Bessie and her friends to the big city.

"I hope the housing allowance will be generous. House prices on the island have gone up considerably over the last few years."

"I don't need much more than a small cottage as it will be only me staying there. I did suggest to Harry and Charles that they might stay with me sometimes, but neither cared for the idea. They prefer the Seaview."

"It is a lovely hotel. I'm pleased for Jasper that they want to keep staying there."

Jasper Coventry was the manager and one of the owners of the large luxury hotel in Ramsey. Bessie had known him since his childhood.

"Harry was considering looking into hotels in Douglas, mostly for a change of scenery, but we get a very competitive rate from Jasper. That will change, of course, as the weather improves and their bookings go up."

"I believe they're booked pretty fully during the summer months."

"They are. So much so that they can't accommodate us from May to September. I've booked holiday cottages for both Harry and Charles for those months. Fortunately, Thomas and Maggie had availability."

"So all three of you will be staying on Laxey Beach during the summer?"

"Unless I buy a house first."

Bessie frowned. She and Andrew had been friends ever since they'd met at a holiday park in the UK a few years earlier. Although it had been something of an adjustment for her since she'd been on her own since just after her eighteenth birthday, she'd come to enjoy the fortnight each

A SNEAK PEEK AT THE DURAND FILE

month when Andrew was visiting. He had many demands on his time, even when he was on the island, but they usually managed to have at least one meal together each day during his stay. In between the meetings of the cold case unit, they also toured historical sites, spent time shopping, and simply enjoyed one another's company.

She wasn't fond of the idea of Harry and Charles also staying on the beach, although that bothered her less than the idea of Andrew buying a house on the island. Whatever he found to purchase, it wasn't going to be right next door to Bessie's cottage, that was for certain.

"I hope you won't mind having Charles and Harry as neighbours," Andrew said.

"Of course not," Bessie replied, even though she wasn't certain how she felt about the idea.

Both men were also retired from Scotland Yard, and both were in demand as consultants in their own areas of expertise. Charles specialised in missing person cases and he was often caught up in investigations, even while he was on the island. Bessie felt as if she barely knew the man, even though they'd been working together for several months.

Harry seemed to be making more of an effort to get to know Bessie and her friends, although he also kept to himself for the most part. He was an expert in murder cases, especially the most brutal and violent ones. Although Bessie had spoken to him more than she had to Charles, he'd told her virtually nothing about himself.

"They arrive tomorrow?" Bessie checked as she finished the last of her lunch.

"They do. We'll have the first meeting for this case the day after, on Wednesday."

"And it's murder again?"

Andrew grinned at her. "Murder times two," he said in a dramatic voice.

"Oh? How awful."

Andrew frowned. "Of course, it is quite awful," he agreed.

"Two murders, but only one case?"

"Actually, it's two cases, but if we solve one, we'll have, more than likely, solved them both. And that's all I'm going to say for today. You'll have to wait for the meeting on Wednesday to learn more."

Bessie frowned. "I've half a mind to not give you any pudding," she replied.

"What is pudding?"

"I made a Victoria sponge."

"You know the others in the group will be quite cross if I tell you anything in advance."

"You could at least tell me one or two interesting things," Bessie suggested as she cleared the table. She cut them each a generous slice of cake while Andrew did the small amount of washing up and made them each a cup of tea.

"One or two interesting things," he said as Bessie put his cake in front of him. "The murders took place in France. The first one happened in ninety-one and the second one occurred two years later. It's possible that the second death was suicide, but, having read the files, I don't believe it. We'll be focussing our efforts on that second death for reasons that I'll explain on Wednesday."

"Now I'm sorry I asked," Bessie said with a rueful grin.

"Let's talk about houses, then," Andrew suggested.

"How many will we be touring today?"

"The estate agent sent me the details for over a dozen properties. I selected four that might be possibilities. I'm not certain how many of them he's actually arranged for us to see, though. He's going to meet us at the first property and we'll go from there."

"What's the name of your estate agent?" Bessie asked as

she remembered one of her least favourite people on the island.

"Mike Harper."

Bessie smiled. "I don't know him at all."

"You sound happy about that."

"I've had some dealings in the past with a very unpleasant estate agent named Alan Collins. I was worried that he was the one with whom you were working," Bessie explained.

Andrew shrugged. "I simply stopped at one of the agencies on the high street in Douglas and asked for information. Mike was happy to send me the particulars for everything he could find to my flat in London."

"So where are we going first?"

"A small bungalow in Ramsey. I requested Ramsey, Laxey, and Lonan. There's a good deal more available in Ramsey than anywhere else."

"It's a large town, as opposed to a small village. I'm sure you'd enjoy living there, as there is a great deal more to do there than in Laxey."

"As my primary reason for coming across will continue to be the cold case unit, I don't know that it matters, really. But the house is reasonably priced and seems to be almost exactly what I need."

Bessie looked around her kitchen. Her cottage was small and some might consider it cluttered, but she couldn't imagine living anywhere else. The only thing she truly desired was more space for books. Her many shelves were full and she didn't have any more space to put in additional storage.

Half an hour later, nicely full of tea and cake, she and Andrew were on their way to Ramsey. When they reached the outskirts of the town, Bessie read through the directions on the sale listing.

"It's a left here and then a right at the end of the road," she told Andrew. "And then the house is the last one on the left."

Andrew parked on the street in front of the small bungalow. "It looks less well maintained in person than it did in the photos," he told Bessie.

She looked at the sales listing sheet and then at the house. "I would suggest that this photo is several years out of date," she told him. "Or that it's a photo of one of the neighbouring properties."

All of the houses along the street were very similar and Bessie spotted two on the opposite side of the road that looked nearly identical to the one with the "For Sale" sign that they were planning to tour.

"Let's hope the inside is better maintained," Andrew said as he and Bessie walked up the short walkway to the door.

Andrew knocked and a moment later, the door swung open. Bessie's heart sank when she saw the man in the doorway.

"Ah, good afternoon. I'm Alan Collins. You must be Andrew Chessman," he said brightly.

Andrew glanced at Bessie and then looked back at Alan. "I'm Andrew Cheatham," he said, enunciating very clearly.

"Ah, yes, of course. And you must be Mrs. Chethham," Alan replied, looking at Bessie. "I'm afraid I don't shake hands. It's a, well, I simply don't."

"I'm Elizabeth Cubbon," Bessie said frostily. "We've met before."

"Have we? I am sorry, Mrs. Stubbon, but I'm terrible at remembering faces. I never forget a property, but I struggle to remember people," Alan told her.

"You showed me a flat on Seaside Terrace in Douglas," Bessie replied.

"On Seaside Terrace? I don't remember ever showing anything in that building. They had a spot of bother there a few years ago. Are you quite certain it was me that showed you the flat?"

Bessie nodded tightly. "I'm quite certain. You showed me a few other properties in Douglas, as well."

"Did you buy anything?" he asked bluntly.

"I decided not to move from my cottage on Laxey Beach," she told him.

"Cottage on Laxey Beach? Treoghe Bwaane? That I remember. The cottage is in a terrible state, really only fit to be torn down, but the land it's sitting on is worth a fortune," Alan said.

"That cottage is my home and it's a very comfortable home, thank you very much," Bessie said tartly.

"You've lived there for sixty odd years, haven't you? It's all coming back to me now," Alan said.

Andrew looked at Bessie's face and quickly interrupted. "I thought Mike would be meeting me here," he said.

Alan blinked several times and then shrugged. "He had another appointment for the same time, so I agreed to come up here and show you a few places. This is an excellent family home in a desirable neighbourhood. The schools are excellent."

"My children are all well past school age," Andrew said dryly. "I'm retired and I'm really looking for somewhere quiet where I can relax and enjoy not having to go to work every day."

"It's a very quiet neighbourhood," Alan said quickly.

"Aside from all of the children taking advantage of the excellent schools," Bessie suggested.

"Oh, they aren't that good," Alan laughed. "But come and have a look around the house. It's ready for new owners, although you may want to do some modernising."

Bessie looked around the small sitting room and frowned.

"It needs new carpets, a fresh coat of paint, and there seems to be a problem with damp in that corner."

Andrew looked where she was pointing and sighed. "I'm not interested in buying a property that needs this much work."

"It's all cosmetic," Alan argued. "The kitchen is spacious." He turned and walked into the next room.

Bessie and Andrew exchanged glances and then followed him slowly.

"It's spacious, but everything in here needs replacing," Bessie said as she looked around the kitchen. The counters were sagging and badly stained. The door to the refrigerator was hanging sideways from only one of the two hinges. The microwave's door had a huge crack running across it and the hob was covered in what appeared to be half an inch of old grease and grime.

"The cooker is nearly new," Alan said a bit desperately.

Bessie opened the cooker's door and then slammed it shut again. "Something died in there," she announced.

Andrew laughed. "This house is definitely not for me. Let's go look at the next one."

Alan nodded. "Of course, not every house is perfect for everyone. I think you'll find, though, that this house is very good value for money. House prices on the island have increased dramatically in the past few years. With your budget, you aren't going to be able to get something completely updated."

"Maybe I'll have to reconsider my budget, then," Andrew said.

Alan handed Bessie the particulars for the next house, which was only a short distance away. Unfortunately, it was another small bungalow badly in need of updates.

"I do think you could save everyone a great deal of time and effort if you were more honest in your listings," Bessie told Alan after they'd discovered that the kitchen cabinets, countertops, and appliances had all been removed and never replaced.

"The listing does say that the kitchen could do with modernising," he replied.

"Except there isn't a kitchen," Bessie argued. "There's just a room that used to be a kitchen."

"The next property has been partially updated," Alan told them. "The location isn't as convenient, though. You should probably follow me so that you don't get lost."

"If you have the address, I'm fairly certain I can find it," Bessie replied.

Alan handed her the listing and she read the address and then the directions to the property. "I've no idea where this is," she admitted reluctantly.

Alan nodded. "Exactly. It's very difficult to find. Some buyers consider that a disadvantage. If you'll follow me, I'll take you there."

Bessie and Andrew got into his rental car and then waited as Alan climbed into the small car with the name of his estate agency written across the door. He drove past them slowly and then stopped at the end of the road so that they could catch up to him.

"We both might have birthdays before we get there," Andrew muttered as Alan drove incredibly slowly through the streets of Ramsey.

"The directions on the listing start on Kipling Street. I've no idea where that is, but once we get there, we should be able to follow the directions and leave Alan behind," Bessie suggested.

They drove out of Ramsey and then turned down a single lane road that Bessie had never even noticed before.

"Is this Kipling Street?" Andrew asked.

"I didn't see any signs. It may be Kipling Street. If it is, we'll be turning left shortly."

After what seemed to be several minutes, Alan stopped and then turned right. Bessie and Andrew exchanged glances.

"Maybe this is Kipling Street," Andrew said with a sigh.

They were still trying to work out where they were in relation to the directions they'd been given when Alan stopped his car on the road in front of a long driveway. The house was completely hidden behind a row of tall trees and shrubs but the "For Sale" sign had been carefully placed right on the edge of the road in front of the trees.

"I think the first thing I'd do is cut back the trees," Bessie muttered as she got out of the car.

"I was thinking the same thing. Unless the house is set quite far back from the road, the trees will be blocking all of the light to the front of the house," Andrew said.

Alan was standing at the bottom of the driveway. "I feel as if this is going to be the perfect house for you," he told Andrew. "It's quite tucked away, behind the trees. You'll have total privacy."

They'd taken only a few steps up the drive when Bessie noticed the smell. "Does anyone else smell smoke?" she asked.

"The house has a wood-burning fireplace," Alan told her. "Perhaps the current owners lit a fire for your benefit."

"Or, maybe not," Andrew said as they finally moved behind the trees and the house came into view.

"The house is on fire," Alan exclaimed. "It's a fire. Fire, fire, fire." He kept shouting the word over and over again as he ran back down the driveway to his car.

ALSO BY DIANA XARISSA

The Isle of Man Cozy Mysteries

Aunt Bessie Assumes
Aunt Bessie Believes
Aunt Bessie Considers
Aunt Bessie Decides
Aunt Bessie Enjoys
Aunt Bessie Finds
Aunt Bessie Goes
Aunt Bessie's Holiday
Aunt Bessie Invites
Aunt Bessie Joins
Aunt Bessie Knows
Aunt Bessie Likes
Aunt Bessie Meets
Aunt Bessie Needs
Aunt Bessie Observes
Aunt Bessie Provides
Aunt Bessie Questions
Aunt Bessie Remembers
Aunt Bessie Solves
Aunt Bessie Tries
Aunt Bessie Understands
Aunt Bessie Volunteers
Aunt Bessie Wonders

Aunt Bessie's X-Ray
Aunt Bessie Yearns
Aunt Bessie Zeroes In

The Aunt Bessie Cold Case Mysteries

The Adams File
The Bernhard File
The Carter File
The Durand File

The Isle of Man Ghostly Cozy Mysteries

Arrivals and Arrests
Boats and Bad Guys
Cars and Cold Cases
Dogs and Danger
Encounters and Enemies
Friends and Frauds
Guests and Guilt
Hop-tu-Naa and Homicide
Invitations and Investigations
Joy and Jealousy
Kittens and Killers
Letters and Lawsuits
Marsupials and Murder
Neighbors and Nightmares
Orchestras and Obsessions
Proposals and Poison
Questions and Quarrels

Roses and Revenge

Secrets and Suspects

The Markham Sisters Cozy Mystery Novellas

The Appleton Case
The Bennett Case
The Chalmers Case
The Donaldson Case
The Ellsworth Case
The Fenton Case
The Green Case
The Hampton Case
The Irwin Case
The Jackson Case
The Kingston Case
The Lawley Case
The Moody Case
The Norman Case
The Osborne Case
The Patrone Case
The Quinton Case
The Rhodes Case
The Somerset Case
The Tanner Case
The Underwood Case
The Vernon Case
The Walters Case
The Xanders Case

The Young Case

The Zachery Case

The Janet Markham Bennett Cozy Thriller Series

The Armstrong Assignment

The Blake Assignment

The Carlson Assignment

The Isle of Man Romance Series

Island Escape

Island Inheritance

Island Heritage

Island Christmas

The Later in Life Love Stories

Second Chances

Second Act

Second Thoughts

Second Degree

Second Best

Second Nature

BOOKPLATES ARE NOW AVAILABLE

Would you like a signed bookplate for this book?

I now have bookplates (stickers) that I can personalize, sign, and send to you. It's the next best thing to getting a signed copy!

Send an email to diana@dianaxarissa.com with your mailing address (I promise not to use it for anything else, ever) and how you'd like your bookplate personalized and I'll sign one and send it to you.

There is no charge for a bookplate, but there is a limit of one per person.

ABOUT THE AUTHOR

Diana started self-publishing in 2013 and she is thrilled to have found readers for the stories that she creates. She spent her childhood and teens years wearing out her library card on a regular basis and has always enjoyed getting lost in fictional worlds.

She was born and raised in Erie, Pennsylvania, and studied history at Allegheny College in Meadville, Pennsylvania. After years working in college administration in both Erie and Washington, DC, Diana moved to the UK following her marriage.

While living on the Isle of Man, Diana had an opportunity to earn a master's degree in Manx Studies, focusing on the fascinating history of the island. Eventually, she and her husband and their two children relocated to the US, where they are now settled in the Buffalo, New York, area.

She also writes mystery/thrillers set in the not-too-distant future as Diana X. Dunn and Middle Grade and Young Adult fiction as D.X. Dunn.

Diana is always happy to hear from readers. You can write to her at:

> Diana Xarissa Dunn
> PO Box 72

Clarence, NY 14031.

Find Diana at: DianaXarissa.com
E-mail: Diana@dianaxarissa.com

Printed in France by Amazon
Brétigny-sur-Orge, FR